Where the White Fricks are
Copyright Courtney Taylor
Published by C. Taylor Books
Courtney Taylor asserts all moral rights over this work of fiction.
 ISBN: 978-0-9941605-3-9
First edition 2023

Where the White Fricks are
by Courtney Taylor

In memory of my grandpa, John Taylor, who when seeing an outraged representative on the evening news, would cheekily imitate their sentiment by saying, "You can't say *that*."

And for my grandma, Beverly Taylor, who proudly procured Albert Namatjira's autograph when he used to come in to Alice Springs' District Office.

And I'd better mention the Sunday School teacher who first taught me about idols.

"Think of the grandeur that once was Rome's, the glory that belonged to Greece. Amongst these ruins are monuments and fragments and magnificent temples erected to their gods... man is a worshiping creature irrespective of colour, language or clime." – David Unaipon, the aboriginal bloke on Australia's $50 note.

Part I

The ORAU

I

The tribesmen danced around an upright wooden pole decorated with eagle feathers, marsupial tails, and blood obtained by piercing oneself with a large splinter. Their black bodies covered with red ochre and white clay, their matted hair constricted by headpieces made of fur-string and leafy twigs, they looked like burnt trees that had shaken free of the rusty soil. However their dance was far from liberated. If they failed to perform their secret ritual perfectly, they would jeopardise the replenishment of the animal they were spiritually connected to.

These initiated men were the direct descendants of a gigantic kangaroo creature. Having emerged from a dim and distant past, it had, like all other ancestral creatures, died and left a landmark. This landmark shared not only the spirit of these men, but the spirit of the object they danced around, and the spirits of the kangaroos they sang about. In the minds of these arid land people, those four things – landmark, object, person, and either animal or fruit – were so connected that each was essentially the other. The repetitive incantations said as much, and called for an increase to the fauna that would nourish the cycle they all belonged to.

The words of the song and the movements of the dance had been prescribed by ancestors immemorial, and were presided over by elders who exhibited an extraordinary degree of control. If a performer made a mistake, correction was immediate, and often achieved by nothing more than a frown. The elders were creaky, leathery old men, white-bearded and covered with thick self-inflicted scars. Some of them were magic men, which meant they could heal people, and hurt people, and even kill people – using nothing more than softly-spoken words. Their understanding of the mystical forces governing the natural world was unparalleled, hence the anxiety of one of the performers.

Several nights ago, a nineteen-year-old named Crijjibah Clibe had stolen away from the tribe's campsite, and in the dark and scrubby wilderness, built a group of fires, reflective of a stippled pattern high above the world. He'd done this because several weeks before he'd remembered a story told to him by one of his uncles. It was about people the colour of teeth, who knew magic that could make a person's head explode. These people, called the White Fricks, lived in a faraway country, but they travelled across the sky every night. To illustrate this, his uncle had pointed at a crescent of white dots moving amid the stars, and said, *See? Das dem up dere.*

When Crijji had remembered all this, and asked the elders about it, they'd scowled and said the pattern was actually a flock of birds that had flown too high and gotten stuck because of the desire to know everything. The warning was implicit and obvious, but Crijji, unable to stop thinking about the White Fricks, had finally ignored it.

And now, as he danced with all the others, in a ceremony to conjure more of their kind, he increasingly feared that his actions had aroused the anger of malevolent forces. Horrible demons lurked in the nighttime darkness, plotting mischiefs that were frightening to think about. In all likelihood those devils had influenced Crijji to light his treacherous fires, and had already told the elders about what he'd done. The elders were probably waiting patiently for the right moment to accuse him.

Crijji grew aware of the force generated by the dancing men around him, and shuddered to imagine himself being knocked to the ground and trampled by their stamping feet. Their crowd was a swirling, constricting mass, its power surging from one person to another as they flowed around their sacred form. These men were his tribal family, but if they learned of what he'd done, the affection and trust would slip from their eyes, and they'd straightaway consider him deserving of death.

Crijji hoped his secret would not be revealed... but the dread growing inside him screamed it would be. And soon.

II

One of the children had apparently seen him wander away into the darkness. They'd said this to someone, who'd said it to someone else, and in no time at all a gathering of hardened eyes had formed around him.

Whadjoo bin do, Crijjibah? one of the elders quietly asked.

Crijji's heart began pumping clots of dead blood. Something rotten marinated in his stomach. It took only moments for the truth to pour of him, as profusely as the sour sweat suddenly coating his entire body. Looking round at familiar faces, he saw people who had instantly become foreigners. Their regard of him had been transformed by a new understanding: Crijji had broken the Law. For this there must be punishment.

Men of every totem comprised the party that would execute justice. They ventured far from the tribe's campsite, making sure that Crijji didn't try to escape. He was too terrified to try something that futile. Shaking so greatly that his legs folded beneath him, he often times had to be hefted to his feet and made to walk onward.

The men came to a stony clearing. As twilight took hold of the world, the elders deliberated Crijji's punishment.

Death, whispered an aged representative.

Crijji didn't understand. Hadn't they meant a spear in the leg, or a blow to the skull? Surely they hadn't meant the ultimate punishment. But they had – as he'd known they would. And all the men agreed with it. Crijji had dabbled with dark and sinister forces. The havoc he could bring upon the tribe, particularly if no reckoning took place, was frightening to contemplate. His body went completely numb, as though poisoned by some kind of venom. The men approaching him seemed to be made of stone. Their every footstep thudded heavily.

A ring of strangers tightened around Crijji, some holding up flaming sticks. There were men of the plum tree totem, the frog totem, the rat, goanna, eagle, quoll, snake and sun and water totems. The grim act of violence they demanded was an ancient custom of atonement called payback. It would ably stem further chaos, and Crijji could do nothing but submit to it.

Crijji's breathing was so fast and shallow that he was practically choking. Tears so clotted his eyes that he felt he was trapped inside a mirage. Not wanting to know who had been charged with the stab or strike that would end him, he lowered his face and prepared for death.

But then, something strange happened – quickly yet with bewildering slowness. The men were suddenly screaming and pulling back their wooden weapons. They were shouting at things in the darkness – things that Crijji couldn't see. He could discern rough and thrashing forms, leaping, crawling, or flying. There were hundreds of them, their eyes like watery gems. When they momentarily emerged into the frenzied light of the tribesmen's torches, they revealed themselves not as hideous demonic forms, which he'd expected, but as...animals.

All around the tribesmen were kangaroos and dingoes, emus, lizards and screeching birds. Worst of all, there were snakes, sluicing through the sand like channels of fast-moving fluid. Crijji, paralysed with terror, could only watch as King Brown snakes, one of the most venomous types in the world, slithered directly toward him, their glistening numbers so great that he couldn't comprehend them.

The hideous reptiles stopped when they were close to him, their black eyes fixed on his. Their waxy heads rose in unison, and the front half of their bodies lifted off the ground. Opening their mouths, they revealed tiny gummy caves and specks of poison-filled enamel. As one, and in Crijji's language, they hissed, *Run*.

A crashing wave of clawing goosebumps lifted Crijji onto his feet and propelled him. He sprinted past his would-be executioners and into the darkness beyond them. Their screams faded but he kept on running, his lithe body carrying him over sharp rocks and prickles that he barely even noticed. He ran for what felt like forever, at first as lightly as balsa, but eventually as heavily as granite. He finally collapsed and lay on the ground, his feet lacerated, his demented, traitorous blood smashing against the insides of his skin. Diseased and burrowing thoughts addled his mind and saturated his body with both grief and confusion. The people he'd left behind – his tribe members – would be devoured by those demon-infested animals. Crijji had left them there to die.

Crijji was a traitor and a coward, and he could never return to his people. This he knew more deeply than anything else. Biting the flesh of his hand, he sobbed.

III

Crijji wandered through weather-worn mountain ranges, valleys that eroded the soles of his feet, and waterless gaping plains that seemed to be endless. The sky had no remorse. It constantly reinstated itself, day after week after month, bringing either unfeeling blueness, or a thin wedge of star-filled darkness and cold that briefly interrupted the hot and dusty monotony.

As he waded through a droning relentless routine, he deeply wished the payback had been carried out, and would envision himself buried inside a small grave, tucked up knees to chest, the women of his tribe standing around it, howling and slashing themselves in grief. Or maybe that wouldn't have happened, owing to how he'd proven himself to have no shame. Shame was like a sense of honour. A person who had no shame was a person with no respect or self-respect. It was a tribal custom not to speak a dead person's name for a distinct period of time. Crijji felt that period should be extended eternally for someone like him. He with his total lack of shame deserved to be forgotten.

His first night alone was terrible. In fact his every night alone was terrible. It was abnormal for a tribes-person to be so isolated. Native people spend every moment of their lives together. Crijji couldn't stop thinking about his family: The women with their lewd jokes; the old people who moved as though their joints needed greasing; the fresh-faced, tangly-haired children who scampered so quickly it seemed their feet were zapped by the ground... He missed them so much that he wanted to die. Of course, night after night and all throughout the day, his mind exhumed the reason for his exile. He'd been a fool to think the White Fricks were real. And his defiance of the elders had been insane. What had he been thinking? And what was he, now that he didn't have his people and his totem? The answer was obvious: he was nothing.

The events of that long-ago night, when his tribe had purposed to kill him but the animals had come, were so bewildering that magic could be the only explanation. Certainly those animals had rushed to his rescue because they'd been commanded to by a magic man. Such wizards were able to see things from a great distance, and powerful enough that they could intervene without being near. Crijji often got the feeling they were watching him even now. He'd actually encountered evidence for this.

On a hateful day fused with all the others, Crijji, too tired to walk, too dispirited to even stand, had crawled beneath the shade of a saltbush tree, his stomach a cave that was gnawing at his insides. Above him, high in the blue sky, there was a circling blur that he knew was a wedge-tailed eagle. He happened to be watching as it dropped something: an object that plummeted, and struck the earth nearby. It was a dead possum, ready to skin, cook, and eat.

IV

On the horizon of a foreign country – a country devoid of recognisable landmarks – Crijji saw an endless row of strange objects. They looked like skinny, flat-topped teeth, and continued east and west in countless numbers. He finally arrived at them, and learned that they were perfectly-straight bones, waist-high and embedded in the ground. Only... they didn't sound like bones. He rapped his knuckles on one and heard a noise unlike any he'd ever encountered.

Suddenly, the objects screamed at him, saying, *Dere bad spirid oba dat way, you keep goin, dey gun gedjaaaaa!!!!*

Crijji bolted so quickly that his own spirit had to catch up with him. Crouched defensively, he watched the bones intently, knowing undoubtedly that they demarcated two different territories.

If magic men were aiding him, perhaps they were using these markers to direct his course. But which way did they want him to go? East or west?

Crijji thought about it for a long time, and finally decided upon west.

V

The man standing next to the markers had glowing rainbow hair that was blowing around like grass underwater. Certainly this person was a magic man. However, he looked about the same age as Crijji. Was it possible for someone so young to be a wizard?

Had Crijji not felt himself to be supernaturally aided, he would have fled the moment he spotted this strange person. Suppressing fear that wanted to make him scream and convulse, he instead treaded toward the man respectfully.

The magic man saw him approaching, and was surprised. Crijji in turn was surprised. He thought the magic man would have expected him.

As per tribal custom, both men avoided eye contact as they established who they were and where they were from. Crijji spoke his own name and the country he was from, of course failing to add that he was an exile from it. An awkward pause lingered for a moment. Both men understood how unusual – and indeed suspicious – it was for a tribesman to be alone, particularly so far away from one's country. The magic man didn't seem too worried, though. He said his name was Albad Abbad, and that *this* was his country.

You mean... oba dere... is your country? asked Crijji, referring to the land beyond the markers.

Albad shook his head in the negative, and replied, *Das where all dem White Carnds is.*

It took Crijji a moment to translate Albad's meaning. When he understood it, there kindled inside him a sudden hope, and a feeling of vindication.

You mean...oba dere lib...people ooz white?

Albad clucked his tongue in the affirmative.

Proper white?

Proper white-as, bruss, replied Albad. *I'm doin business wi' dem carnds. But dey not biggin ub.* He raised an object he was holding. It looked to be made of mica, and had a shape that was totally unnatural. Crijji staggered backward when it suddenly lit up with colour. *Das ow we talk,* added Albad.

You a... magic man? asked Crijji.

Albad nodded, then broke into a smile and clucked his tongue, saying, *Nclaaaair.* It meant he was only kidding.

Den ow come you... Crijji pointed at Albad's glowing rainbow hair.

Albad, realising what Crijji meant, reached up to his own scalp and pinched at something. His hair returned to its normal black colour and fell down over his face. *I bin god dat prom White Carnd*, he said, holding out something small for Crijji to take. *Das d one I do business wib.*

Crijji received the object, which was like a small beetle without legs. Prompted to by Albad, he placed it onto his own scalp, then peered curiously at the mica object. It took a few moments for Crijji to figure out what he was looking at. The person in the mica... it was him. That was *his* hair dancing around like a multi-coloured bushfire!

Crijji's face must have been filled with wonderment, because Albad, with a knowing expression, said, *You wan' see em eh, dem buckin White Carnds. I'll show you, coz dey all comin to our ceremony tonight.*

VI

The eight other performers of that ceremony were waiting close by, amid a galaxy of flies – airborne melanomas they never once swatted at.

Ay Albad, said one of his cousins, all of whom were male. *Dat White Carnd bin gib you d al-gol?*

I bin tol'joo, said Albad. *Ee nod 'llowed to. Ee'll get trouble.*

I'll gib im trouble, said another of the cousins. *I'll stig a nulla-nulla right up his ards-ole.* His statement prompted a chorus of dry chuckling, and then hacking to clear out phlegm.

The cousins were lounging on the dirt in various postures, in such a way that they seemed contractually entitled to do so. Crijji was glad that they had little to no interest in the newcomer among them, and noted the men's resentment when Albad said, *We god ged ready. Ee'll be startin soon.*

One of the cousins professorially replied, *Ee god gib us d al-gol.*

Albad shook his head reproachfully, knelt down, and began striking a rock against a flint rock. In not long, the heap of sticks before him had bloomed into a healthy campfire.

When the sun eventually melted away, Albad harried his cousins to their feet, and compelled them to strip down and put on red loincloths. They did, grudgingly, and then daubed white ochre onto their bodies. Crijji became intrigued when realising it wasn't actually ochre, but a gooey substance he'd never before encountered. It came from a container whose material was also foreign to him. There were other strange items scattered across the ceremonial ground, having come, no doubt, from the White Fricks.

In spite of their natural raucousness, the cousins effected an appearance almost regal. White slashes decorated their bodies, along with dots and squiggles that made them seem otherworldly – as if scrawled with an alien language. Albad, who was inspecting everyone's costumes, looked at Crijji and said, *Ay. You wan join in?*

Dis not my ceremony, Crijji replied.

No one's, said Albad. *'S bullchit.*

Marvelling at the strangeness of the situation, Crijji received the container of gooey stuff and daubed it onto himself. Presently, he looked and felt like one of the tribe. Memories of his own tribe, and of real ceremonies he'd taken part in, summoned feelings he quickly suppressed.

Albad produced a pair of short thick sticks and clacked them against each other, creating a staccato beat that his cousins mechanically began dancing to. Crijji didn't know how to respond to their lack of seriousness. It seemed highly disrespectful... but at the same time really funny.

One of the cousins sang, *Dat buckin White Carnd Cregree. Ee god gib us d al-gol, ubbawise we gun bash im, n' stick a big buckin nulla-nulla right up his ards-ole!!*

VII

Several hundred metres away, fourteen pairs of binoculars were trained upon the fake ceremony. Those binoculars had been handed out by a short man named Darren, who, like his boss – the esteemed Tour Guide Gregory Barrett – wore a khaki safari outfit that both enhanced his credibility and bolstered his confidence. The glistening cherry of their uniform was a leather stockman's hat, banded by plastic crocodile teeth. Both Darren and Gregory were known to tip this item with courtesy and regularity, especially toward the ladies.

'Now remember,' whispered Gregory, a tall and balding man with a shiny rosy flush at the top of his cheeks. 'What we're about to see is Secret Men's Business – a mysterious rite of passage whereby a boy becomes a man. And before anybody asks: If I told you what Secret Men's Business is, it wouldn't be secret now, would it.'

On cue, the tourists all laughed. Gregory directed his wobbling head and charming smirk toward a raised hand.

'What are they singing?' asked an Austrian named Lars.

'The songs of their ancestors,' said Gregory, mystically, 'which have been handed down since the Dreamtime. The one at the moment is about living in harmony with the land and respecting the earth. See the native closest to the campfire?'

Thirteen pairs of binoculars reeled around and scanned the ceremony taking place just beyond the white steel border posts. Finally the native in question was located, thanks to his dancing more rambunctiously than the others. Gregory was about to expound upon why this was the case, when, unexpectedly, the dancing native raised a soft drink can and took a satisfying swig.

'Ahhhhhhrrrmm,' said Gregory. 'There are certain parts of the ceremony that, to be respectful of, we should look away from. Watching on is almost akin to– perving.'

Susannah from Switzerland asked, 'What does this phrase *perving* mean?'

'And what was that element the Aborigine just took a drink from?' asked Bartholomew (aka Bart) from Holland.

'A- an element?' said Gregory. 'Ohr the can. Yeah the can. That object is a...ahh...annnn artefact. A residual reminder of...White Man's Pervading Influence. Yeah. The, uh, natives have appropriated it, as a, uh, reminder. Hence why they use it in their ceremonies.'

'Fascinating,' said one of the tourists, who, like Darren and Gregory, hailed from Victoria.

'Or tragic, some would say,' said Gregory, pleased at how well he was pivoting. 'See the soft drink can is now part of their ceremonies. Being hunter-gatherers, they hunted-and-gathered it into their way of life. You see, when Contemporary Australia and Original Australia were first established –'

'Sorry to interrupt,' said Romina from Berlin. 'But is that Aborigine smoking a...cigarette?'

The binoculars all focused upon a painted tribesmen who was grinning, nodding, and taking a deep drag from a small white cylinder pinched between his fingers. A puff of grey smoke flooded out of his mouth.

'Yahhhhr – no,' said Gregory. 'That object is actually a... tree root, that the Aborigi– sorry the Original Australians– have smoked in their ceremonies for thousands of years. And this is actually quite a serious part of the ceremony, so, out of respect, perhaps we should leave them to it, and, uh, retire for the night.'

'*Is* this a serious part of the ceremony?' asked Martin (pronounced Marteen) from France. 'They sound as if they are... laughing.'

'Um,' said Gregory, gesturing for his anxious employee to hurry up and collect the binoculars. 'That laughter is ah, um, it's ah... um... part of their culture.'

VIII

The twelve tourists were sitting on fold-out chairs, around a campfire that many of them almost resented because they weren't allowed to roast marshmallows. On the first day of the tour, Gregory had said, 'We don't allow marshmallows on this tour. Out here, in this country, a marshmallow can kill you.'

Quietly and sourly repeating the reasoning for this edict, the backpackers said:

'A marshmallow can get stuck in your throat and burn your from the inside-out.'

'It can cauterise your oesophagus.'

'There's an eighty-seven percent chance of fatality.'

'Did he actually say eighty-seven percent?'

'No I think I just made that up.'

Nine Europeans burst out laughing. Three Victorians looked up momentarily then returned to writing in their journals.

Several minutes later, the tourists all had their eyes closed, while Gregory, seated with prominence upon a fold-out stool, asked them, 'What do you hear when you listen to the *silence* of this land?'

The soulful question received no answer, because the silence was unexpectedly torn apart by an eerie shrieking and jabbering noise.

Lars from Austria, glad he hadn't been chewing on a hot marshmallow, asked in a voice chubby with emotion, 'What was *that*?'

Gregory stood and fixed his eyes on the rocky silhouettes beleaguering their feeble campfire. The inky hills to the south so captivated him that the wide-eyed tourists began shifting nervously.

Darren, to break the silence, said, 'Could have been the Wild Woman,' and seemed a fraction vulnerable when no one asked him to elaborate on his cultural knowledge.

Gregory pulled himself away from the darkness to the south... and then jolted with fright when his mobile phone rang!

The electronic chirping that pierced the eerie silence again made Lars thankful for the ban on flaming marshmallows. Looking round at his fellow backpackers, he saw them patting their chests in relief, and quietly laughing with each other.

Gregory pulled out his phone, checked it, muttered to himself disapprovingly, then returned it to the pocket of his khaki shorts. Sitting back down on his fold-out stool, he said, 'Y'get things like that, here in the Outback. I remember one time when–'

Suddenly, a black native plastered with white horrible symbols leapt out of the darkness, shouting, 'Buck you, buckin White Carnds!!!!' He swung a stick that cracked Gregory directly on the back of the head. The tour guide fell to the dirt – lucky not to land in the fire – as more natives burst from the darkness.

No matter where the screaming tourists fled, there were crazy-eyed indigenes on all sides of them. Quickly were they mustered back to the campfire, where they sobbed and clutched each other like traumatised children.

Gregory staggered to his feet, rubbing at the back of his head, and said, 'Aw what are ya doin' ya pack o' mongrels! You're not sposed to go past the border!'

'Blbbllblblbllblblbllb al-gol,' said one of the tribesmen.

'What?' said Gregory.

'Blblblblblbllblblblb *al-gol*, you buckin White Carnd!' the man repeated, adding what was obviously an insult.

Bart from Holland, hands in surrender mode, asked, 'Did... did he just use the word *alcohol*? And did he just call you a –'

'No,' said Gregory, firmly, and summoning all the poise he could; 'he did not just use the word alcohol. How could he? He doesn't even know what alcohol is. And besides, it's *illegal* in his country.'

'Blblblblblblblbllb *al-gol*, buckin white dot licka!' said another of the tribesmen.

'I think that *is* what he said, boss,' said Darren. 'I think they *are* after the – '

'They're not!' said Gregory. 'And all of you be quiet while I handle this.' Turning to address the natives, he said, 'Uh... greetings, honourable, tribesmen.'

The next thing Gregory knew he was on his hands and knees, and three malodorous wild men were pulling at his shorts. Were it not for their tightness – and also perhaps the impatience of the natives – those shorts would have fallen.

One of the Europeans gasped and said, 'He's not going to be the same.'

'Whatta ya mean!?' shouted Gregory.

Awkwardly contorting around to see what was happening behind him, he saw that a native had hold of a thick tree branch, and was pulling it back as though about to ram a door with its sharpest end.

'Bloody no! Nooo! I haven't – I can't – I can't give you the alcohol! I could lose my tourism licence!'

'Comparatively, boss,' said Darren, 'that's not too big a deal.'

'I could even go to gaol!'

'Even still,' said Darren.

Gregory thought about the issue for a moment, then shouted, 'Alright! It's over there, in one of the eskies, in the trailer! Darren – bloody show em where the alcohol is!'

Darren broke away from the huddled tourists, and with momentary boldness, began waving like a man directing 747s at a packed children's crossing. 'It's over there,' he shouted. 'Yeht, over there! That's right, over there!'

The untold numbers of traditionally-painted warriors flocked to two 4wd vehicles and the trailers they towed. There was the sound of smashing glass, the wobbly *coonk coonk coonk* of someone jumping up and down on a bonnet or a roof... and then a cry of celebration.

Gregory watched forlornly as the pirates made off with a pair of plastic treasure chests, and could only nod with sadness when one of the Victorians said, 'They took the coffee beans... didn't they.'

IX

The Abbad cousins had been waiting years for this glorious moment. Having grown up on stories about a magical elixir that could make a person feel like they were flying, they'd mythologised it even further by talking about what *they* would do if able to procure it.

Too impatient to wait until they'd made it back to their own country, they ceased bashing their way through the scrub, and dropped the eskies onto the ground. Plonking themselves in a reverent, cross-legged circle, they lifted the lids off the plastic containers, and goggled at the magical items within.

'Buckin ell,' said one of the cousins, holding up a handful of ice, amazed at this thing he'd never seen before.

Some of the men used their teeth to prise off the bottle caps. Others were more inventive. They smashed the neck of the bottle on a rock, then lifted its jagged opening to their smiling lips.

The historic event quickly descended into a heartfelt, sometimes incoherent discussion about what each cousin loved about the other. It was so engrossing that they failed to notice a faint buzzing noise which gradually developed into an overhead roar.

A blinding beam of pale light slammed onto the gathering. The cousins sprang to their feet, shouting, 'Ah! Allichopter!'

Symptoms of dizziness and vertigo affected the cousins as they woozily tried to evade the clutches of the border patrol. Two helicopters hovered above them, each producing a hydraulic arm that groped around to capture them. The method of capture was a glassy box, which had unfolded from a flattened state, thence to trap the men by stamping the earth and absorbing them through its bottom pane.

In less than thirty seconds all of the cousins had been captured, four men to each crystal cube. They bashed on the glass walls of their pen, laughing their heads off, and saying things like, *Elp! Elp! Dey tryin'a rape us!*

The helicopters flew beyond the markers, deeper into Original Australia, and deposited the eight cousins in the middle of the star-covered wilderness. There they sat on the dirt, looking at each other blankly, and then began the inevitable task of allocating blame.

It was decided that a cousin named Arbee was the one to blame, because Arbee was the one who'd come up with the idea to transgress the border and appropriate the alcohol. Arbee of course disputed this, but a majority rule decreed him the culprit.

In the morning, when the sun was obscenely high, the cousins woke with pounding heads and desiccated tongues, and learned that Arbee hadn't received the payback – Mygul had! Mygul was so battered that his face looked to be curdling.

Aw chit! one of the cousins shouted. *Whad dis mean? Now we gotta payback ebryone, coz we bin payback Mygul stead o' Arbee? And Arbee, ee god pay us back, too? Chit!*

The logic was indisputable, and all of them knew it.

For a long time the cousins did nothing but sit there, slouched over, and letting dust creep into every orifice. Then, one of them spotted a faint shadow doing circles on the ground, and looking up, saw a wedge-tailed eagle descending toward them.

The cousin grinned and said, *Us mob, we god breakbaaaaaaasssssttttt!*

X

Albad had tried to warn the White Carnd, but Cregree hadn't answered his phone.

Albad and Crijji had found themselves a decent perch on a hill, and watched the cousins storm the border, harass the foreigners, and then get apprehended by allichopters.

Crijji had never seen anything as magnificent as those machines. He could tell by the way they flew that they were heavy. And the light they shone! It was brighter than the sun – but a whiter colour! He couldn't be certain, but he felt with quiet confidence that he'd just the encountered a closer view of the white dots high above the world.

He soon began to wonder: how had those allichopters known about the cousins?

Cregree, said Albad; *ee bin told me: We got deez fings in ere* – he tapped the back of his own hand – *d White Carnds bin put em dere.*

Crijji was confused by Albad's meaning. Albad said, *Loog, I'll show you.*

Albad produced the mica object, tapped it a few times, and held it over the back of his own hand. Crijji looked at it and tried to understand what he was seeing. It seemed that he was looking at the bones beneath Albad's skin. On top of them, but still under the skin, was a small circular shadow that looked like a splashed tear.

Das why we can't go deir country, said Albad. *Deez fings* – he pointed at the circular shadow – *tell doze fings* – he pointed at the white markers – *and dey all scream ad uz. And when dey scream at us, d White Carnds come!*

Sitting down on a rock, Albad reached into a bag made of a rustling material that Crijji was perplexed by.

Try dis, said Albad, throwing a small object, which Crijji caught and inspected in the moonlight. *You eat it.*

Crijji tentatively bit the object. His face screwed up at the taste of it.

Noaw, said Albad. *You god take opp d wrapper.*

Whad?

Ere, I'll cho you.

Albad received the small item, peeled it apart, then handed back something which had been trapped in a skin. That something, when Crijji bit into it, was the most delicious thing he'd ever tasted. It flooded his mouth with a sweetness unrivalled, and had him asking, *Whad is id? You god more?*

Albad clucked his tongue in the affirmative, adding, *Only coz I bin 'ide it prom ma cousins. Buckin digg-eds, dey scopp ebryding. 'S called Joglud.*

Joglud?

Na wid a Cha. Choglud.

Choglud?

Das right; joglud.

Albad reached into his bag and produced another joglud. He threw it to Crijji, who unpeeled it himself this time. The two of them munched on joglud till there were no more left in the bag. Both needed a drink of water afterwards, what with the parched feeling that resulted.

Crijji lowered the roo-skin bladder that he'd made for carrying water, and looked to the northward distance, the land beyond the white markers. Presently, he asked, *You reckon d allichopters would know ip we go dat way wibout deez?* He tapped the back of his own hand.

Albad, who understood his meaning, and understood the conclusion it would lead to, said, *You wan' cut em out.*

Crijji nodded.

Coz you wan' more joglud, yeah?

Crijji cackled and replied, *I wan' see White Fricks. Proper close.*

You'll be sorry, bruss, said Albad, chuckling. *Dey all ugly ones.*

But Albad quietly thought about Crijji's proposal... then said, *Dad be easy.*

Albad's mica object shone a light that allowed them to see what they were doing. Crijji went first. With a sharpened stone that he used for cutting, he pierced the skin on the back of his hand, ripping it open so the wound was big enough to poke his finger into. After several slippery attempts, he managed to extract a small, bloodied filament that looked like a circular fly's wing.

When Albad had done the same, they buried the objects in the ground, their rationale being that the wind might otherwise blow them beyond the markers and alert the allichopters.

Both young men were nervous as they approached the markers. They stopped just in front of them, and looked at one another, both for acknowledgment that they were doing the right thing. Neither could confidently provide that confirmation, but they stepped forward regardless.

The markers didn't scream when Crijji and Albad stepped past them. Both men were hugely relieved. As well as that, they were excited. Ahead of them was a rumpled foreign country saturated in unfamiliar magic and mythology.

Crijji had a hidden ambition that he was too embarrassed to voice: He wanted to track down some White Fricks, and persuade them to come back to his country, so they might meet his people, and convince them to forgive Crijji for breaking the Law. If the elders could see that the White Fricks were real; that Crijji had been right... surely they'd change their minds about his crime.

Crijji smiled as he and Albad trekked deeper into the White Fricks' country. For the first time in his memory he didn't feel like a ghost, but a real live tribesman, one with a real live tribe to return to.

Part II
The UMCAU
XI

Over the years, United Multicultural Australia, known locally as Zin Kadesh, had bubbled outward till it could bubble no farther. Its outermost tenements were a cliff-face of bamboo scaffoldings loaded with plastic-bag and cardboard-sheet shanties. The never-ending fence surrounding it was five metres high, topped off with electrified razor wire, and mounted with an abundance of armoured surveillance cameras, each inscribed with the acronym COAU.

It was three o'clock in the morning, and Sayeed Mihail, a swarthy twenty-seven-year-old, was watching out for any unwanted witnesses. His offsider – a 6ft3 Sudanese man named Charles Gaco – was wielding a shovel. The pair was one of hundreds, each digging a long trench in a land of dust and opportunity, their excavations each hidden by a tarpaulin canopy. These individuals belonged to a clandestine organisation known as The Society of Cultures for the Expansion of Zin Kadesh. Their current operation had them stealthily transplanting the border fence.

'Hey buddy,' said Charles, pausing to wipe his brow with the hem of his denim jalibaya – a rugged robe that was the members' uniform. 'Do you hear that? It sounds like a, how you say, engine.'

'An engine?' said Mihail, stopping to listen. After a time he said, 'Probably the damn Lebanese. Doing burn-outs and backflips to show off who's got the smallest pollinator. Did you know that in many other countries they're actually greatly respected?'

'I did not, buddy,' said Charles, before asking, 'Do you think we should Get Down and Blankefy?'

'Might be a good idea,' said Mihail. 'That engine seems to be getting closer.'

The two men hurried along the length of their trench, lowering its canopy by collapsing its support poles. When the tarpaulin was level with the ground, they crouched underneath it and peeked out through a slit.

'We've got the lions and tigers to thank for your keen sense of hearing, Charles,' whispered Mihail. 'The only thing my ears are good for is telling how crowded a train is.'

When confident that the vehicle had passed them by, they re-raised the canopy and resumed the transplantation. Mihail said, 'I think a night in a Zin Kadeshi gaol would do them good, Charles. They might lose a few toes or come down with dysentery, but breach the border of any other country and you'd get shot.'

'Hey buddy,' said Charles. 'Who are these people?'

The instinct to make a joke about the phrase *these people* was vanquished by panic that screamed for Mihail to raise his arms in unequivocal surrender. Turning around slowly, he fully expected to see a COAU Ground Patrol. But, instead of lanky robots with turbine guns for hands, all he saw was... nothing.

'What are you talking about, Charles?' whispered Mihail.

'Cannot you see them, buddy? They are not African, but they are very dark. Maybe they are African American.'

Squinting in the region Charles was facing, Mihail noticed a pair of outlines that gradually ripened with definition. Duly, he saw two young black men – lean and clothed in animal-skins – who were gawking at him and Charles, obviously surprised by their emergence from the ground.

'Oh... my... goodness,' said Mihail. 'Charles. Those are the Aboriginalians (no that's not the right word; it's a hyphen); the ones that have escaped from their country. Whatever you do, don't do it quickly. I remember the phrase "potentially dangerous."'

'They have escaped, buddy?'

'And they've been all over the news.'

'Oh,' said Charles, impressed. 'But I do not understand, buddy. Why are they trying to get *in* to Zin Kadesh?'

Mihail realised that Charles was right: the Original Australians (yes that was the right title) were climbing the border fence so as to make their way into the UMCAU. This meant that – he gulped – they were climbing toward the electrified razor wire at the top of it.

'Uh, excuse me,' said Mihail, forced to speak louder than he would have liked to. 'The consequences of what you're doing will be very... consequential.'

'They are not listening, buddy.'

'Maybe *you* should say something, Charles. There might be some solidarity, given the pigmentation.'

'Uh, excuse me, how you say, uh, gentlemen. What you are doing, it is not going to be good for you.'

Charles looked around for a means of emphasising his warning, and found it on the ground. Bending down and picking up a rock, he gently threw it near the Originals to get their attention. This action was instantly deemed offensive. One of them scowled, dropped off the fence, found a rock of his own, and pelted it straight at Charles.

A speeding blur struck the African directly on the forehead. He fell backward like a logged tree, landing heavily against the edge of the trench. Mihail could see that Charles was unconscious, and that the Original was searching the ground for another rock. The native found one, pulled back his arm, took aim, and then –

Bwaaaaaa!

Blinding white lights suddenly swung onto the situation, flashing in sync with a musical beat that was positively blasting. The Original dropped his rock, threw himself against the fence, and climbed it like a taunted spider, straight toward the –

Bk-zzzzzzzzzzzzz-ttt!!!

Shooting sparks accompanied the indigene as he plummeted to the dirt, his limp body sending up a cloud of dust. His friend cried out something in their language and rushed to his side.

Mihail realised that the burning halogen beads were headlights, and behind them was a driver who probably intended to do a "fully sick leap" up and over the border fence. Directly behind the excavated fence post was an alleyway – slim, yes, but the driver was obviously lining up to launch into it.

The vehicle revved its engine and cranked its suspension, then spun its wheels, gained traction, and accelerated toward the trench, reels of dust spewing out the back of it. Mihail screamed something sacrilegious, and grabbing hold of Charles, dragged him fully into the trench, only a moment before the vehicle sprang off the ground like a grasshopper, and *whooshed* over his head.

The off-road racing car sailed through the air, and would have easily cleared the trench and the fence... had it not snagged its front bumper on the tarpaulin canopy. Tent poles ripped out of the ground all around Mihail; and looking up at the naked sky, he saw that the flying car had an extra-long cape with steel pole trimmings. This unexpected drag made it descend heavily and prematurely, right toward the –

Crunch! The vehicle impaled its back axle on the top of the fence post, then bucked forward into a nose-dive as yellow gems of electricity exploded everywhere. The concrete base of the post turned like a ball in a socket before slipping and skidding down the length of the trench. Mihail watched it coming, aghast at being struck by such a hefty block of concrete. But the mesh connecting the post to its colleagues went taunt, and the concrete stopped sliding – only millimetres from Charles and Mihail's faces.

The car, skewered on the end of the post, looked like a shoe hanging on the end of a stick, and was dragging the fence almost to a flattened position. The vehicle, becoming lodged inside the alleyway, had created a zapping wreckage of lashing sparks, one that sounded like an all-in brawl of robotic snakes. Most significantly, it had smothered the dug-out leading back to the UMCAU.

Mihail knew he could do nothing but wait for the arrival of a COAU helicopter. And there it was – a luminescent grain in the eastward distance. In not long it would be here; and if Charles was lucky, his injury would spare him from the squalid confines of the notoriously unreformed Zin Kadeshi prison system.

The conscious Original Australian was looking at Mihail beseechingly – as if imploring him for help. The young man's big and glistening eyes caused Mihail to acknowledge that, in any other circumstance, this native would have made a very valuable asset. Commodified compassion, he believed it was called. He chuckled weakly, as though in shock, and wobbled as he looked around for something – anything – that might help mitigate this unexpected dilemma.

The nearby sparks were igniting like new generations of flaming grasshoppers. Squinting through that plague – at the mangled slope leading up to his home country – Mihail came to realise that the sparks weren't firing from everywhere. There was a blank section; a channel of clear air. This was thanks to the tarpaulin, whose long and syrupy ribbon was like a third-world red carpet laid out over a war zone.

An epiphany slowly dawned – one so encouraging that Mihail ended up shouting what he started out whispering, 'I've been saying it for years, Charles. When Allah closes a door, he builds a bomb and blows open a window!'

Turning to the Original, Mihail pantomimed the intention of picking up one's respective friend and carrying him through the carnage. The Original understood, and obviously thought Mihail was insane. Mihail would have agreed, were he not privy to certain scientific realities.

Mihail bent down, and straining with effort, hoisted Charles onto his shoulders. The African felt heavier than a cow, and was just as awkward in shape. With every muscle burning, Mihail carried his fellow Expansionist up onto the uprooted concrete block. There he contorted his head skyward, and saw that the helicopter was almost directly above them.

'Yalla yalla yalla!'

The comprehending Original scooped up his friend, slung him over his shoulders, and leapt from the edge of the trench, over onto the flattened fence. A moment later, a heavenly white light crashed down onto the trench, and a vertical torrent of wind blasted it like an invisible waterfall.

Clouds of dust choked the air as Mihail and the Original carried their friends across the slanted fence. Sparks were leaping up and biting them, but at least the men weren't being electrocuted. The tarpaulin covered the electrified razor wire, insulating them from its angry energy. Ordinarily this probably wasn't possible, but the tarp in question was covered with a clotted paint, to help texturise it and make it blend in with the landscape.

At the end of the fallen fence was a drop about two metres high. Beneath them, horrible music was pumping, and someone was screaming, 'Aw muh Gawd! Muh car!' Mihail looked back and saw precisely what he feared: four spindly machines that looked like elongated Rottweilers. They'd leapt out of the helicopter and were loping down the trench. They sprang up onto the fence and aimed their front limbs.

'Forgive me, Charles!' shouted Mihail, as he unburdened himself of the heavy African. Without pausing to think, he pushed the conscious Original, so that both he and his friend also tumbled into the dusty alleyway.

And not a moment too soon.

Whizzing past Mihail came a silver bracelet, programmed to latch onto a wrist or ankle and detain a person. More followed, fired from the arms of border-bots. They lacerated the air all around Mihail, and – *whoops* – caused him to lose his footing.

The sky and the ground competed for Mihail's attention, and then – *hooooiiii* – the air rushed out of him when the planet bodily slapped him. He found himself lying on top of Charles, and staring at the car's driver: a man who had crawled out of his upside-down vehicle. The man's gold chain and brand-name clothes confirmed Mihail's guess that he was a wealthy Zin Kadeshian (probably Lebanese) who had jumped the border fence for the thrill of doing illegal burn-outs in a foreign country.

Rolling onto his back, Mihail looked up and was blinded by the glare of the helicopter's spotlight. Gouged out of it were the skinny silhouettes of the four border-bots. They were perched on top of the pinned car, their sinister heads (which resembled ergonomic bike seats) aimed directly at him.

But then, as one, those heads all panned in the same direction, and fixed their attention upon the two Original Australians. Mihail could tell what the machines (or the people operating them) were thinking. Smiling and getting to his feet, he dusted off his jalibaya and said, 'One must know one's jurisdiction. Mustn't one.'

The four canine heads snapped sideways and fixed him with a glare. He slightly wilted under the ferocity of it... then ducked in shock when a flaming object smashed against one of the robots.

Outraged Zin Kadeshians of all heritages were emerging from their shanties, many clutching weapons of an impromptu variety. More flaming bottles flipped and shattered and sent out waves of flame. Some of their lit rags must have been wadded-up flags, because, in spite of the focused animosity, the Zin Kadeshians quickly forgot about the border-bots, and began fighting among themselves.

Harried by a bickering ocean of turbans, robes, cricket bats and fists, Mihail found the conscious Original, who was protecting his friend, and communicated via his hands that they needed to get out of here. The Original evidently felt the same way. He picked up his friend and waited for Mihail to do likewise with his.

When Charles was slumped over Mihail's shoulders, the latter led the way through the surging, rollicking crowd, away from the collapsed fence and the now-flaming car beneath it. A round of machine gun fire suddenly erupted! The entire mob hunched and tried to scatter, but couldn't, due to the tightness of the alleyway.

Mihail heard a *ping* coming from his pocket, and knew right away that the app which warned of neighbourhood collapses was warning of the present vicinity. 'Ohhhhhh not good,' he said, adding spice to his step. 'Yalla Yalla Yalla!' he yelled, his voice one of thousands suddenly shouting the very same thing.

One side of the alleyway began slanting as if being pushed over. Wooden slats slid off their bearers and clattered onto the ground. Styrofoam boxes filled with black market organs pelted down and clobbered people. Mihail braked when a cage full of flapping chickens hit the dirt and burst open in front of him.

'Follow the chickens!' he heard somebody shout. For a moment he almost did, but then thought, *What?*

A horrifying noise began sounding behind them. It was a cracking noise, like gunfire. The bamboo struts of the tenements were bending like rubber stalks and snapping near their bases. One side of the alleyway broke, fell toward the other, and smashed against with it. By some method of divine deliverance, the crowd in the alley wasn't crushed, because as the two walls fell simultaneously, a triangular tunnel was somehow created. Joyously yet frantically everyone sprinted through it. They stampeded out of the alleyway and into the street beyond. As both tenement structures came tumbling down, the last straggler *just* made it out of the alleyway, amid a cloud of white dust that was either gyprock residue or cocaine.

The Zin Kadeshians watched the wreckage settle into a dusty mound of debris. Covered in white powder that rendered them all equals, they looked at each blankly, and then burst out cheering. People who ordinarily would have hated each other, hugged each other, and shouted and jumped about like party-goers, despite the fact that all of their possessions and many of their loved ones were likely buried in the rubble.

Already people had begun fossicking for valuables. Normally Mihail would have been alongside them (hence the alert on his phone). But this occasion was different. His *valuables* were different. Looking at the conscious Original, he said, 'Alright, it won't take long for the authorities to broker an agreement, whereby...' Realising the native had no idea what he was saying, he swatted at his own stupidity and said, 'Just... follow me.'

He turned and proceeded through the jubilant powdered crowd, habitually looking back to see if the Original was still following. He was. Mihail smiled. Unable to quite believe that such fortune could have been lavished on him, he marvelled at the possibilities, and led the way deeper into United Multicultural Australia.

XII

An entourage of beggars hurried alongside them, babbling through electronic translators that looked to be made out of soft drink cans. The multi-linguistic chattering was put to an end by a pair orphans brandishing grubby syringes. Mihail and the conscious Original hurried on, leaving the parties to settle their grievance among themselves. Guaranteed there would be casualties; if not now then eventually. Territorial disputes over begging rights were known to get quite vicious.

Clogged sewer pipes shook and rattled inside claustrophobic mud-brick canyons. The sky above – a sooty slit – rotated to a new angle whenever they turned a corner. At a certain point inside the grimy labyrinth they came to a grated, muck-filled water catchment. Mihail lifted the grate, reached into the muck, and emerged with a plastic fishing tackle box.

'Wah!' yelled Charles, startling to life, courtesy of the torn paper packet held beneath his nostrils. Looking around with wide, terrified eyes, he eventually calmed his breathing and said, 'Oh buddy. I thought I was back in refugee camp. That place was horrible. Where are we? And why is my head hurting?'

'We're at the checkpoint, Charles. And your head is hurting because that sleeping fellow through a rock at you.'

'He threw a rock at me?' said Charles, peering at the unconscious Original, and squinting as if trying to recall a distant memory.

'He did. And it's why I'm hesitant to wake him. His friend seems more reasonable, however.'

The conscious Original Australian was crouched next to his unconscious friend, and was stealing glances of Charles and Mihail as they conferred. Understandably, the Original seemed nervous.

'What are we going to do with them, buddy? They do not seem very... ordinary.'

'Charles, I believe the celebrity of these two gentlemen might well aid our plight. And I don't just mean the plight of us two – I mean of *all* Zin Kadeshians.'

34

'Oh,' said Charles. He refrained for a moment, but then said, 'Will the Society agree with you?'

Mihail felt his stomach drop. Horrified, he looked at Charles and said, 'I forgot to send out a warning on the group chat.'

'Oh no,' said Charles, his eyes widening. 'Do you think right now everybody is being... arrested?'

'I... I don't know,' said Mihail, his mind stumbling over its thoughts, his hands shaking as he checked his phone to see if anybody else has sounded the alarm. It seemed nobody had. The last message on file related to a broken shovel.

'If the COAU was to arrest everybody,' said Charles, cringing at the idea, 'they would not go to a COAU gaol; they would go to a Zin Kadeshi gaol.'

Mihail nodded, and stammered, 'That's the deal.' Double-checking the group chat, he said, 'Should we warn them now?'

'Is there a reason why you would not?'

'Well,' said Mihail, weakly, 'if you and I are the only ones who haven't been arrested, and we send a message now, people might be angry that we didn't send out a warning sooner. Some transgressions are worthy of a severed head. This perhaps is one of them.'

'*I* would want to risk it, buddy. The COAU has found the trench that *we* have dug. They will want for to find every other one. If everybody is not arrested yet, they will be *soon*.'

'So I should send out the warning? Even though it will mark us as the ones who failed to act?'

'I think you should, buddy.'

'Alright then, Charles. Here's to our heads. May they always remain attached.'

Mihail typed the word *BREACH*, added three exclamation marks, and pressed send. He held up his flashing phone to Charles, who, ever gracious, only chuckled nervously.

'I suppose,' said Mihail, numbly, 'we must proceed as though the worst has taken place. Let us assume, Charles, that our fellow members have all been discovered, and are right now being detained.'

'There are so many of them, buddy,' said Charles. 'If the COAU government gives them to Zin Kadesh, will the prison system not... explode?'

'So what should *we* do, buddy, if, how you say, these two people can help everyone?'

'Well,' said Mihail, 'I believe we can leverage their clout. If the COAU government learns we have in our possession two of its beloved Original Australians, they might well submit to our demands. Charles, I propose to you, that we *might* just be able to gain clemency for our friends; and who knows, perhaps even get the border expanded *legally*.'

'Ooh,' said Charles, impressed. 'How would we do that, buddy?'

Mihail smiled and replied, 'By embracing tradition, Charles. By featuring these two individuals in a hostage video.'

XIII

Disguises were procured by pilfering garments from sagging overhead clotheslines. The pegs clamping them shrieked in protest, and the owner of the clothes erupted from his elevated shanty and gave a mostly-naked chase. It ended when the man trod on a puddle deeper than he'd thought it to be, fell upon his face, and was set upon by a pack of bony mangy dogs.

When the unconscious Original was awoken by the same method as Charles had been, Charles and Mihail patiently waited for him to get used to his surroundings, and then encouraged both him and his friend to don some new attire. The Original was distrustful. However, after speaking with his friend, it was clear that they both understood the purpose for the black dresses. Their disguises were completed by wrapping burqas around their faces.

Zin Kadeshi buses had a habit of exploding, so instead of taking public transport (which would have been packed even at this early hour) they rented a Tuk Tuk. The three-wheeled motorbike with a hard-topped roof puttered to the vending machine where they'd bought their tickets. Mihail climbed onto the driver's seat; Charles onto the seat next to him; and the Originals onto the backseat, as if being chauffeured. *Chaperoned* was a more appropriate term, because Mihail had appropriated a white robe and a red-chequered keffiyeh, for the purpose of appearing to be the male supervisor of three women. (Charles' disguise was a purple sari and a floral hijab). As Mihail revved the tinny engine then pulled back on the throttle, he felt himself to be quite the ladies man.

The rising sun poured thick orange light onto a lumpy, far-reaching panorama of corrugated iron, domes made of packed-mud, and rusty antennas that hackled away into the dense tobacco haze ever choking Zin Kadesh. Grungy electrical cables seemed to moor the city so it didn't float away to become space junk. So too did its tangled array of elevated roads, often made of concrete, but just as often made of wood, like old-time roller coasters. In all directions these looping arteries were clogged with smoke-pumping traffic. Most vehicles were so corroded they looked as if they were habitually parked in salt water.

Because all parties were hungry (or at least looked to be) Mihail veered onto a rickety pier whose wooden boards made a *tooka-tooka-tooka-tooka* noise as they drove over them. Not for the first time he wondered if this was how Tuk Tuks had earned their name.

Foregoing the more ethical establishments (whose fluorescent signs avowed things like, *No msg, No animal adrenaline, No cat dog monkey*) Mihail motored toward a vending cart that looked like an ice cube hatted with the iron roof of a beach hut. Inside it, protected by scratched-up bullet-proof glass, was a tired-looking woman nearing the end of a twenty-one-hour shift. Receiving their orders then cooking them, she slid, through a battered steel drawer that looked as if someone had bashed it with a crowbar, styrofoam boxes filled with Mexican food.

'This is a good choice, buddy,' said Charles, handing a box of food to both the Originals. 'Everybody likes Mexican food.'

'Indeed you seem to be right, Charles,' said Mihail, watching the two natives devour the food. 'They look as if they've never eaten anything more delicious.'

'I think they are just very very hungry,' said Charles, prising off the tab of a fizzing drink and then passing its can to the Originals. The two men in burqas flinched at the sound of the bursting can, tentatively sipped its contents between themselves, compared views, and hurriedly downed the rest of the liquid till there was nothing left – not even droplets. Charles smiled and said, 'You were right, buddy. They do like the orange flavour.'

Self-drive mode allowed Mihail to eat without distraction. Munching on something that hit the spot with a sledgehammer, he said, 'It shouldn't be too hard to write a script for a hostage tape. One can probably even download a template. But you *are* sure your friends will have the necessary props?'

'I am yes quite sure,' said Charles. 'They are very well protected. And I think they will be happy for us to film there. They all have to go to work in the daytime, so the house will be, how you say, empty. Their house is a very nice one, too. They bought at a time when it was cheap, because there were a lot of rapes going on in the neighbourhood. But now there are not so many rapes, because the rapists sold their houses, and made enough money to go and live somewhere else. But for some reason it is still called Somali Town.'

Their road pitched forward and descended into a vast, layered depression, zig-zagging from one populous land platform to another, heading deeper into a pit shaped like a giant inverted Aztec temple. These steps were leading them into a suburb known informally as The Holy Land.

XIV

Above the ground's surface the Dirt Scraper was a squashy oriental frontage with a crumbling pagoda roof. Beneath the ground's surface it was a crude stack of accommodation levels 127 metres deep. Abandoning the Tuk Tuk, the four disguised men proceeded down a widely spiralling staircase that wrapped around the structure's diametre. To their left was dirt retained by a translucent glaze. To their right was crowded level after crowded level, each of them little more than creaky wooden boards laid over steel floor-bearers embedded in the surrounding soil.

'I wish we could take the elevator, said Charles, leading the way past naked lightbulbs and rusted iron beams. 'But not very long ago, a man who is very, what is word, fat, made the whole thing stop working. Sometimes also it is hard to breathe down here. This is because the... the...'

'The ventilation system?' offered Mihail.

'Yes, the ventilation system. It is not very good. Is powered by sewerage. My friends do not like the whole idea of it.'

The remark was apostrophised by a sudden stench that made Mihail want to hold his new keffiyeh over his face. Waiting outside a communal bathroom was a long queue of people. Their grimaces made it clear that cutting the line was a death-worthy offence.

At the fourteenth level they exited the stairwell and padded down an unpainted (but graffitied) gyprock corridor. Stopping at a wooden door with the number 419 scrawled onto it, Charles knocked, and waved at a tiny lens no bigger than a pinhead.

'Do not worry everybody,' he reassured them. 'My friends are not connected to the Society. And they are very friendly people.'

The door swiftly opened, and out of it came the barrel of an AK-47 – an antiquated but still very effective machine gun. Standing behind it was an African in his thirties. His head was shaved, his expression grim. To the three veiled women and the short brown man chaperoning them, he said, 'Yes?'

'Miebaka. It is me, Charles. How are you going?'

'Charles?' said Miebaka, showing a crescent of pearly white teeth. 'Why are you dressed like a woman? And who are these other women?'

'They are not women, buddy. And is a very crazy story. Can we come in?'

'Of course, my man,' said Miebaka, lowering the gun and holding open the door.

The tiny one-room dwelling was filled with boxes, suitcases, buckets, and fifteen other Africans, male and female. Sitting on beanbags or lying on the floor, they were all eating porridge and wearing identical bright red T-shirts. Having heard that the man in the sari and the hijab was their friend Charles, they said, 'What is going on, Charles? Are you not coming to work today? You have not gone Musvestite, have you?'

'No no no,' said Charles, waving away their concern. 'It is nothing like that. Some people are chasing us and they are not very nice people.'

'So this is where you come to hide?' said a lanky, deep-voiced African named Pubuda . 'You and your Musvetite friends?'

'Pubuda,' said Miebaka. 'You know Charles better than that. He would not put us in danger. And they are not Musvetites anyway.'

'What do you mean they are not Musvetites,' demanded Pubuda. 'Look at what they are wearing. *Those people* view *these people* as *abdominations*. We are just *asking* for someone to throw a grenade through that door.' He said something in an African language. Miebaka replied in that language. Pretty soon there was a sixteen-person foreign-language debate, so heated that Mihail edged backward for the door. One of the Africans pointed this out then scornfully motioned at Pubuda. Pubuda lifted his hands, wobbled his head, and added an African sentence to what was obviously, 'It's not *my* fault that –'

The debate ended when Pubuda folded his arms and said, 'Fine. I don't care. I was just putting it up for discussion.'

That statement lit *another* fiery foreign-language debate, which abruptly ended when Charles unwrapped the hijab from around his head. All of the females gasped, and in unison, said, 'Charles! What happened to you?'

Remembering that there was a solid lump on his forehead, Charles prodded it tenderly, wincing as he did so. Evidently overwhelmed by the concentration of attention, he said, 'Uhhh... somebody threw a rock at me.'

'*Who* threw a rock at you?' asked a chorus of indignant female voices.

'Uhhh... he did,' said Charles, pointing at one of the burqa-wearing men. 'Or it might have been the other one.'

Every head in the room turned toward the two Originals. After a lengthy pause, Miebaka treaded closer and quietly asked, 'Charles. How well do you know these friends of yours?'

'Friends?' said Charles. 'Oh. This one is Sayeed, a friend from... a good long time ago. The other ones we just met today.'

'You just met them today?' said Pubuda. 'It is six o'clock in the morning. How well can you know them?'

The debate sparked by *that* statement ended when somebody said, 'What are they going to steal? The floorboards?'

'Charles,' said Miebaka. 'Do you believe these people are trustworthy?'

'Of course, buddy. Would I bring you here people who are not?'

Miebaka turned around to canvas a consensus. The only African who didn't nod or shrug was Pubuda, who folded his arms, shook his head, and muttered inaudibly.

'I suppose it is alright for you to stay here today,' said Miebaka, at last. 'We have all been rostered onto the day shift. If you see any mice, please kill them. They are very filthy creatures.'

The clock hit 6:25, the Africans threw their porridge bowls into a bucket and made for the door. As his fifteen flatmates filed past him, Miebaka said, 'We will be back at seven pm this evening, hopefully with leftovers. But I think there are some in the icy box; please help yourselves to them. Of course it is not much more than crumbed poultry.'

'Thank you, buddy. But we just had breakfast not quite long ago.'

'The midday meal is important, too,' said Miebaka, philosophically. 'Alright. I had better go – before I tell you what that bump on your head looks like. Haha!' He turned to leave but then said, 'Oh. And do not worry about Pubuda. He is just like that because much of his family was killed in a genocide.' Miebaka gave a toothy grin, waved goodbye, and closed the door.

'This place is perfect, Charles,' said Mihail, taking off his keffiyeh. 'And you were right about the weapons. In one of those boxes there's a machete for every resident. We'll have to get your friends a gift basket. But first!'

Mihail plonked onto a beanbag and brought out his phone. After tapping it several times, the glassy rectangle beamed a holographic news article. Charles sat down nearby. The more they watched and listened, the more they cringed and groaned.

The new caster said:

'At approximately 3:25 this morning, Contemporary Australian authorities uncovered what might be considered evidence of the turmoil within United Multicultural Australia. Over 450 men and women, claiming allegiance to an organisation known as The Society of Cultures for the Expansion of Zin Kadesh, were caught in the act of "transplanting the oppressive symbols of the COAU government." Effectively that means they were stealthily relocating the border fence.

'It's not yet clear how the plot came to be unveiled, but authorities have released the names and images of two men believed to be responsible. Charles Gaco and Sayeed Mihail are currently wanted for questioning by several branches of the UMCAU government. The men are advised to hand themselves in as quickly as possible, to thereby avoid the retributions of their own organisation.

'COAU border police are often rounding up would-be illegal immigrants, who in the hope of a better life attempt to escape the country established to provide that life. But never before has a collective so large –'

Chilling images showed the border-bots wrapped around people in jalibayas, constraining their arms and legs with their own arms and legs, and doing their walking for them. Mihail fast-forwarded the article, forcing its reader to hurriedly say, *'But-although-the-conflict-ridden,-heavily-populated-nation-may-be-groaning-under-its-own-weight,-that-isn't-to-say-its-borders-haven't-already-been-extended.-On-five-different-occasions-in-the-last-three-decades,-UMCAU-representatives,-hoping-to-restore-their-country-to-the-"Wide-Open-Nation-State"-it-was-intended-to-be,-have-been-successful-in-their-appeals-to-be-granted-more –'*

Impatient with the usual coverage of smoky skirmishes, riotous funerals, wailing women and children in bandages,

Mihail switched off the article, saying, 'They're not telling us anything we don't already know, Charles. And did you hear what they said about the "retributions of our own organisation?" That was a threat.'

'I agree, buddy. From someone in the Zin Kadeshi government. The corruption is very, how you say, high up in the air.'

Nodding at the burqa'd Originals, Mihail said, 'These two gentlemen caused all this trouble. We need to draw upon that knowledge when we give our performances.'

XV

Two bearded men wearing flowing white robes entered the Dirt Scraper and proceeded down its stairwell. Kareem, who had the thicker beard, said, 'Remember, Hassam. No one will be here save for the plan-revealing infidels and a pair of Musvetites. That means we don't have to worry about killing any women or children.

'Not that we *would* be worried about killing any women or children.'

The two Expansionists gazed at each other for an extended moment before bursting out laughing. As they descended to the fourteenth level, they held their breath whenever a gaggle of residents approached, and dusted off their robes when that gaggle had passed them.

Stopping at door number 419, they leaned in close and heard, 'If our demands are not met, the wards of your country will face consequences you will regret for all of said country's history. We demand an immediate pardon for all Expansionist members who...

'You know you might be right, Charles. It might be more effective if we speak in gibberish and just have English subtitles.'

Kareem and Hassam gazed at each other before bursting out laughing. Realising they'd forgotten themselves, they stifled their laughter, resumed their listening, and learned that the voices on the other side of the door had gone quiet.

Making intense eye contact, they both nodded, and reached into their respective pockets. Kareem emerged with what looked to be a steel credit card. Hassam brought out something that looked like a translucent golf ball.

'For our brothers, my brother,' whispered Kareem.

'And our sisters, my si... brother, ' replied Hassam.

'Yaaaahhhhhhhhh!!!!' shouted Kareem, as he inserted his lock-cutter in between the door and its sill, and thousands of screeching sparks leapt out.

Hassam leaned back then booted the door. It flew open and he ran forward with his arm pulled back, ready to throw his pressurised air bomb. But before he could do so – *Bk-zzzzzzzzzzzttttt!!!!!* – A-crouching-figure-wearing-a-black-balaclava-darted-forward-and-jammed-a-taser-against-his-testicles!

'Sweet Animal!!!!' screamed Hassam, jolting on his feet like a tap dancing rag doll. He spun in several circles, tripped, and embedded his head in a gyprock wall.

Before Kareem could even laugh at the fact that Hassam was kneeling like a headless supplicant – *Bk-zzzzzzzzz-t* 'Yaaaahhhhhhh!!!!' – an unholy pain grabbed hold of *his* testicles. Tearing himself away from the agony, and flailing like an orangutang, he turned and sprinted down the corridor, so quickly that his prayer cap leapt off his head.

Kareem arrived at the stairwell; and to be crafty, went down instead of up. His ploy would have worked had his pursuers not seen it happen. They followed him down the stairs, the verminous infidels; he could hear their echoing footsteps. But never would they catch him. The curling downward path strobed beneath his feet like something immaterial. The human obstacles flowing toward him were virtually insubstantial. Kareem had so transcended the physical that he almost felt he could leap into the air, with his arms out in front of him, and *soar* the rest of the way down.

Plodding up the stairs came a funeral procession, holding up the shrouded body of a young man who'd died of Typhoid fever. Kareem saw a glorious, divinely-provided opportunity. Shoving his way into the somber crowd, he grabbed the corpse by its wrapped-up head and *yanked* it downward. The body slammed head-first onto the stairs and crumpled into a perfectly suitable roadblock.

'Ha hah!! shouted Kareem, as cries of shock and bewilderment whirligigged past his ears. With a graceful spring or an elegant side-step, he dodged any attempt to molest him, and continued down the stairs – happily *un*molested.

The mesmerising trail of steps eventually concluded. At the bottom level of the D-scraper Kareem faced two options, and speedily chose the one that required him to again reach for his lock-cutter. Slicing through the deadbolt of what appeared to be a maintenance access, he hefted back its heavy door and ran into a darkened room. Its lights flickered on automatically, and Kareem learned he was surrounded by large whirring machines. They looked like over-sized car engines, and had large glass cylinders pumping some kind of brown bubbling sludge.

A cascade of angry mourners flooded down the stairwell and into the engine room. Men with bulging eyes wielded chair legs, belt buckles, walking sticks, and anything else that could be swung. Some were enraged enough to only need their teeth. They changed their intentions, however, when Kareem reached into the pocket of his white flowing robe and produced a pressure bomb.

Invigorated by the sudden terror of his would-be attackers, Kareem pulled back his arm and shouted, 'Allah u Akbar!' He went to pitch the air bomb, but instead, it slipped through his fingers and fell toward the floor like an oversized sweat drop.

KABOOM!!!!!!!!!!

Kareem did a double backflip and slammed against a concrete wall, thrown by a misty flash that bodily rocked the pumping machines. Before the mourners had time to laugh, their faces compacted in disgust, because a fetid chocolate mudslide sluiced across the floor toward them, at a speed that made them hopscotch out of the room in desperation.

Kareem's eventual return to consciousness took place in a vat of diluted excrement so deep that his feet could hardly touch the floor. Finally remembering who he was, where he was, and what had happened, he waded out of the engine room then swam toward the stairwell. The stairs were blocked off by a thick glass wall, behind which, insultingly, was an avalanche of furniture, placed there no doubt by the disgruntled mourners.

Never mind, thought Cunning Kareem (as he quite often called himself). I'll take the elevator.

'Damn!' he shouted, when learning the elevator shaft was also blocked off. The glass walls must have been part of a security system, deployed when his bomb had gone off. The panels had completely sealed the lowest level, likely to prevent the recycled waste from contaminating the rest of the Dirt Scraper.

Kareem was chest-deep in rising waste, and, oddly, hoping that security cameras were recording all this. For he was about to prove himself one ice-blooded escapologist. Producing another air bomb (which, luckily, hadn't gone off in his pocket), he waded a few steps back and sank down into the liquid. When his head was totally submerged, he raised his arm and pulled it back, blindly gauged the direction of the glass wall, and ditched his pressure bomb with such strength that he baptised his throwing arm entirely.

BOOOOOOOIIIIIKKK!!!!

A momentary crater opened up in the sewage before crashing back onto itself and completely shattering the glass wall. The marsh poured through the opening and dumped Kareem into the elevator shaft.

Breaking the surface of the rising bilge, he heaved and blinked as though having been maced (which he previously had been – several times, in fact). When finally able to use his eyes, he spotted, in spite of the low light, protruding rungs that ascended up the inside of the shaft. Kareem grinned, waded over to them, and began climbing.

Glass panels blocked off level after level. Until... about ten floors up... one of them was open.

Kareem ascended to it and hauled himself over its ledge. Rolling onto creaky wooden floorboards, and wavily standing to his full height, he saw flashing ceiling lights, and heard an automated multilingual message telling people to evacuate. A small giggling *heh* escaped the Expansionist. He'd looked ahead and seen a door scrawled with 419.

Kareem stalked down the corridor, his muck-saturated robe plastered to his bony body, his hand reaching into his pocket for the last of his pressure bombs. Kicking open the broken door marked 419, he stepped inside, and jumped in fear when a grumpy old Asian woman swung a machine gun and aimed it at him!

With the keen eyes of a predator, Kareem assessed the situation. Hassam's hands were raised pathetically. His face was covered in white powder, and there was an oval-shaped hole in the gyprock wall behind him. Through that hole snooped *another* grumpy old Asian woman, pointing a harpoon at Hassam's head.

'W-what's that smell?' said Hassam, sounding like a man dying of thirst.

'It's the stench of Hell descending upon you,' said Kareem. 'You and your ancient harlots. Who *are* these aged buzzards?'

'They are the neighbours. They've been told to shoot me if I move.'

'And *have* you moved?'

'No.'

'Coward.'

'Please, Kareem, they are not to be trifled with.'

The old woman proved this by tightening her grip on the machine gun and barking out a directive. The condescending sentence was in a language the Expansionists didn't speak. Its meaning, however, was obvious: put down your weapon and sit next to your friend.

Kareem shook his head in the negative and said, 'Put down *your* weapon, grandmother. Otherwise...' He let go of the pressure bomb, but deftly and softly caught it. Hassam deflated in relief; Kareem shook his head in recrimination.

'This tired old bladder isn't going to shoot us,' said Kareem, staring hypnotically at the old woman. 'I see it in her eyes. She's terrified.

'Hassam! Where are the men we have come to kill?'

'These old women,' said Hassam, 'they have a nephew. He is allergic to many things. He lives inside a plastic bubble, and has a card that allows him to use the elevator in an emergency. The infidels have helped carry all of his equipment up to the surface. Not all of it. They are coming back down for more.'

'And we will be waiting for them,' said Kareem. 'Hassam. Reach into your pocket and tell me: how many air bombs do you have left?'

'Two,' he presently replied.

'The third is lying on that beanbag,' said Kareem. 'You must have dropped it.' (He added that with scorn). 'Go and pick it up, and use all three air bombs to sever access to the stairwell.'

'You... you want me to...'

'To blow up the floor, on this level, directly in front of the stairs. Those infidels will not escape this building.'

The eyes of the old Asian woman further narrowed. Kareem could tell that, behind those slits was a reptilian brain of the coolest order. He had lied about seeing terror in her eyes. If anything, here at last was the steely adversary he had always longed for. He wondered if she was married.

As Hassam gathered all the air bombs, left the unit, and made a floor-shaking explosion, not once did Kareem and the old Asian woman break eye-contact.

'It's done,' said Hassam, on returning. 'Not even an African could leap that gap.'

'One of them *is* an African you fool,' said Kareem. 'And two more of them *might* be.'

Kareem used the influence of the pressure bomb to ease his way out of the unit without getting shot. The old woman treaded in pursuit of him, her machine gun never wavering. Kareem was yet more impressed.

Arriving at the elevator shaft, he told Hassam to reach into his (meaning Kareem's) pocket for the lock-cutter, and to cut through the rungs in the shaft. 'If those infidels try to climb their way out of this mess, they'll be unhappily surprised.'

Sparks flew as Kareem and the old Asian woman stared each other down, stopping when Hassam swung out of the elevator shaft and said, 'I think they're coming.'

The other old Asian woman had hurried forward with her harpoon. Obviously they were sisters; they shared the same disagreeable glint. Kareem wondered if it was against the righteous law to marry a pair of sisters.

Emanating from the shaft came a *tktktktktkttktktktk* noise. Kareem understood it when a caged elevator stopped a fraction beneath the floor of the corridor, and the four people inside it swayed about like people on a raft. The elevator was operated by a motor winch, through which ran a chain. The controls for it were held by a short brown man wearing a red-chequered keffiyeh. This infidel raised his arms when spotting Kareem. Kareem motioned for him and his Musvestites to exit the elevator. They did.

'You people disgust me,' said Kareem, taking a few lingering moments to survey the contours of the three Musvestites. 'Hassam! We leave!'

Kareem and Hassam both stepped into the caged elevator, Kareem seizing the controls. Before pressing the Up button, he said, 'Would you like to come with us, grandmothers? There is room in the harem.' He wobbled his head as the charming are wont to do, and shrugged philosophically when the weaponised women gave no reply. 'We leave,' he said, with finality.

The elevator ascended inside the shaft, making the same *tktktktktktktktk* noise. Glass panel after glass panel, up, up, up... And then... An obese Caucasian in his fifties, staring hungrily at their ride. He'd managed to slide open the glass panel and was waiting for the elevator.

Kareem pointed squarely at him and said, 'Don't you even think about it.' He held up his pressure bomb but to no avail. The obese man swept open the gates of the caged elevator and stepped inside. The entire thing dropped and started bouncing. The motor winch stopped *tktktktktktk*-ing, and made a horrible steely straining noise.

The obese man grinned in a demented porcine way. Behind him, waiting to step inside the elevator, were glum children of various heritages. Kareem suddenly understood the dynamic. This fat kafir was a pervert, living in the UMCAU because of the strength of his native country's dollar. The children behind him were his property. This sort of thing was common in Zin Kadesh. Turning a blind eye to it was cultural.

'Look at it this way,' said the obese in man, in a dry CO-Australian accent. 'If that bomb of yours manages to kill me, you won't be able to get me off this elevator.'

Before that logic could be acknowledged, the winch snapped and the elevator plummeted. Kareem, Hassam and the fat CO-Australian squealed as floor after floor whipped past them. Finally, the elevator slammed onto bilge that was harder than concrete. Its floor bottomed out and the fat man went with it, feet first and disappearing into a dark warping bog. He was followed by Kareem's pressure bomb, which had floated in front of their eyes the whole way down.

Boooooiiiikkkkkk! was the noise the bomb made as it detonated under the sewage. It threw up a mound of brown liquid that shoved Kareem and Hassam against the elevator's ceiling. Breaking through a trap door that flung open as they hit it, they were free of the caged elevator as it sank into the murk.

Kareem's first gulp of air almost made him vomit. Hassam was also struggling not to cough out his gizzards. Dolefully they treaded rotten water, neither with the energy to climb the ladder leading to freedom, and seeing no point in doing so anyway. Hassam had chopped off the rungs at level 14. They would have to wait either for the sewage to rise above those mutilated rungs, or for the building to collapse, in which case they would meet a quick and merciful death. How they would explain the circumstances of that death to their peers in paradise... it was something neither wanted to think about.

Kareem and Hassam gazed at each other, both trying to be stoic, and to hold back tears. Finally, Kareem managed to say, 'Let us be joyful in knowing the infidels will also perish.'

Suddenly, a large transparent beach ball struck and divided them one from another! Inside that ball was an old Asian woman, no longer with a gun, but definitely possessing a smirk.

More of these orbs followed – five more, in fact. In each of them was a different person: another old Asian woman, a Musvestite, another Musvestite, a tall Musvestite, and then the short brown chaperone in the red keffiyeh. Their plastic bubbles so crowded the elevator shaft that they stacked on top of each other. Worst of all, they pushed Kareem and Hassam under the sewage and gave them little space to raise their heads and breathe.

'Pop them, Hassam!' screamed Kareem, his voice gurgling. 'Pop them!!'

Both men were clawing at the plastic bubbles to deflate them but were having no success; the plastic was too tough. Kareem gnawed with his teeth but couldn't gain traction.

And then, an ominous noise rumbled above. It sounded like a gargantuan locomotive pounding its way closer. Kareem knew instantly what it was. It was the sound of the Dirt Scraper's armature collapsing. The floors outside the elevator shaft were giving way and crashing down onto each other. A vertical avalanche of accommodation levels had begun.

Iron platforms loaded up with wooden planks and the possessions of countless families thundered down the pit, accreting their way past the ullage in the elevator shaft. They continued on until their final *slam* created not only a shockwave of sound, but a jet of sewage water that blasted violently up the shaft.

'Alllahhhhh!!!!' screamed Kareem and Hassam, the dense channel of waste lifting them at such a gut-lurching speed that the girders of the shaft thrashed past them like square tracks around a bullet train. There was light at the end of this square tunnel. It was accompanied by a noise that sounded like the gurgling belch of a gigantic lard-throated demon. They were rocketing toward the ground level – the sweet, bountiful ground level!

The six plastic bubbles and the two Expansionists smashed through the pagoda roof, the former sailing like grapes shot out of a cannon, the latter flipping through the air amid a universe of chunky brown clots. The crowd assembled on the street outside dissolved in certain places. Of course, Kareem and Hassam descended from a great height and landed in those places.

Kareem struck the pavement and found himself looking up at the sky. As well, glistening bubbles danced before his eyes, bouncing across a sea of raised hands like beach balls at a rock concert. The people inside the bubbles were happy. So were the mud-spattered people holding them up. Evidently it was something of a privilege to be raising those bubbles high. People were so enraptured that they seemed not to notice the effluence coursing around their ankles. That said, people often crapped in the streets in the UMCAU. It was cultural.

XVI

The rusty train ploughed through a vast tent marketplace, the canopies in front of it folding down to make way for it, the canopies behind it rising so that unschooled underage apprentices could resume haggling. Sitting on the carriage roofs were hundreds of individuals, among them Charles, Mihail, and the two Originals. They were on their way to a place where Mihail could think without distraction.

The train didn't even slow when it came to a wooden jetty grafted to the tenements encircling the marketplace. Jumping out its doors or dropping off its roof went patrons who hit the deck either running or rolling. The Chaperone and the Chaperoned were among them.

A grubby glass office complex was cantilevered above a staunch concrete wall pockmarked with bullet holes and grenade blasts. Inscribed above an arched entrance was a multilingual sign reading, *The First Botanical Gardens of Zin Kadesh.*

Caged turnstiles durable enough to separate gorillas gave them entrance to a crowded parkland. Above it was the underside of the office complex, painted blue in order to simulate the sky. Another attempt to create a sense of vastness could be glimpsed in the surrounding forestland. Its trees were broadcast from elsewhere, and displayed on the park's inner walls thanks to pixel paint. Cramped and smothered was the general feeling. That the blue paint was faded and flaking, and the pixel paint was bruised where people had battered it, lent the sanctuary a sense of neglect.

At the centre of the park was a small pond, and at the centre of the pond was a sizeable water feature crusted with algae and patina. The first citizens of Zin Kadesh were commemorated with a statue that depicted a rickety fishing trawler. Standing on its prow was a man pointing valiantly into the distance. Behind him was a huddled mass of people, many clutching babies. Thanks to internal pipes, streams of water coursed down everybody's cheeks.

As Mihail committed himself to conjuring a new action plan, Charles kept the Originals occupied by showing them around the park. Mihail was thankful. He had lots to think about. Zin Kadesh wasn't safe anymore (not that it ever *had* been safe); they needed to get out, and quickly. But how? Even if they made it all the way to a COAU city, they'd be immediately sent back to Zin Kadesh. The only other option caused Mihail to laugh sardonically: They could escape to the ORAU and live with the Originals. Even then, though, they'd probably be hunted down and extracted. The Originals were something of a protected species.

Charles and the two Originals were standing at the base of a Lebanon cedar, looking up at its peak, which pressed against the ceiling and curled over. Mihail could empathise with the poor tree. He too felt squashed by the city. It was constricting like a diabolical python, and their only hope of properly escaping its grip was by appealing to the masses beyond it.

'Gaining support is imperative,' he murmured. 'Even if at first they hate us... As long as they talk about us. What we need is... a symbol: Something for people to rally around. And something with enough magnetism to draw people's eyes away from those Originals. *Vying to be the Vulnerable* is what we'll doing. But what could be more vulnerable than a poor old Abori...'

The entire world suddenly wrenched into pristine focus. Looking over at the water feature, Mihail saw a preponderance of bronze babies held up by tired and hungry-looking statues. He knew immediately that he'd found his symbol. Although...

'Would that be considered plagiarism?' he said out loud. 'Even if it *is* – so what? You can say, *The Campaign for Compassion Continues.* (Or was it *Crusade*? No it wouldn't have been that; too many negative connotations). But honestly,' he said, with a chuckle. 'What trustier tool than the tried and true?'

In less than a minute his entire plan was staring him in the face, like some kind of divine beatific messenger. He could hardly believe it; and with a tone of voice conveying that sentiment, he looked at the bronze trawler and said, 'All aboard the HMAS Victimhood.'

'BUDDY!' yelled Charles, a note of fear in his voice. 'WE HAVE TO GET OUT OF HERE!'

The tall African in the hijab and sari was sprinting across the patchy grassland, the Originals right behind him. One of those Originals had dislodged his burqa: his entire face was on display.

A loudspeaker suddenly blared, *'All botanical units, we have a vertical misdemeanour in the woodlands. I repeat, we have a vertical misdemeanour in the woodlands.'*

Mihail began running in the same direction as the others, who caught up to him in moments. Together they sprinted for the exit, Charles saying, 'One of the ticket inspectors, he wanted for to bribe. But I had no money. Then he wanted to, how you say, have relation favours – with that one. But he saw it was not a woman!'

Emerging from behind shrubs and trees and even splintery park benches came men in navy blue uniforms – probably part of an extortive family monopoly, what with their similar weak black moustaches. Unholstering tasers they raced alongside the quartet, firing electrified barbs that struck grass, tree, or innocent bystander, but thankfully never the intended targets.

The Pursued and the Pursuers raced for the turnstiles, barging through clumps of people who were doltish enough not to step out of the way. The gates spun like heavy propellers, and would certainly break one's neck if one hit them at breakneck speed. Mihail cringed, threw himself forward, and was blessedly surprised when he and his Musvestites passed as one poetical unit through the very same gate, which swept around and ejected them onto the bustling street outside.

Their smooth and highly unlikely transition from chaos to calm couldn't be celebrated for too long. Looking back, they saw that the ticket inspectors were lodged inside the turnstile thanks to a wedged baby's pram. The five or so ravenous men were trying to fire their electrified barbs beyond their jurisdiction. The barbs went off, struck the mesh of the gate, and a thousand starry sparks erupted.

'Let's get out of here!' shouted Mihail.

Nearby the parkland was an enclosed marketplace – an ad hoc surge of development that looked like a construction site wrapped in tight industrial plastic. A sagging chain bridge took them to one of its middle levels, where a pair of murky rubber-sheet doors opened into a cool, partially dehumidified shopping warren. It was a gridded, multi-levelled maze of what looked to be inner-city fire-escapes all growing over each other. These iron balconies and staircases were loaded heavily with purveyors of anything cheap and tacky. Mihail felt grateful for the crowd... until he saw his own visage beamed onto the overhead vault of vapour. He and Charles were wanted fugitives.

It wasn't long before a beefy man with a glistening scalp and a hairy neck was casually following them and muttering to himself. Mihail was certain he was a security guard, alerting an authority as to their presence.

This proved true when a sinister-looking object hovered overhead, aiming a glassy bulge in its belly at the crowd below. The drone, about the size of a lawnmower, looked like a fly doing the splits with extra-long legs. Mihail considered it their cue to move on to quieter pastures.

They exited the shopping complex via the same kind of rubber-sheet doors but at a different location. Blasted by the mid-morning heat of a Zin Kadeshi day, they came face to face with another drone. This one said, '*Stop in the Name of the Law.*'

'I wonder if that line has ever worked as intended,' said Mihail, before throwing up his arms and sprinting.

A crowded wooden boardwalk continually bifurcated into a network of timber paths that looked like a family tree laid flat over a shanty estate. The advantage of the drones (because soon there were eight of them) was not having to stick to any of the boardwalks. Where the quartet had to turn a corner and run till the next corner, the drones simply had to veer slightly in a new direction. It was obvious they wouldn't shake the drones like this. The machines were too many and too quick, and they themselves were too restricted. They needed to get off this wooden labyrinth.

An option presented when they ran alongside a rusting rectangulist mountain-scape – a choppy blocky vista of shipping containers stacked on each other. There must have been thousands of them. The closest was almost reachable. Charles skidded to a stop and said, 'Buddy. We can make it there.'

'*You* can make it there,' said Mihail, horrified. 'You're African.'

'I believe *anybody* can,' said Charles. 'Except for unhealthy people. And you are not unhealthy.'

Charles climbed up onto the creaking guardrail, crouched like a surfer, then sprang, soared, and *cong*, landed heavily on the flat roof of somebody's house. That somebody – an irate man clutching a knife – threw open a trapdoor and started barking, but Charles flipped the trapdoor back onto him – *cong* – and stood on it.

'Come on, buddies!' shouted Charles. 'You can make it!'

The burqa'd Originals were up onto the guardrail then over onto the rooftop before Mihail could even protest. Charles looked across the expanse and shrugged, essentially asking, Are we to leave you here, buddy?

The drones were pressing in close like bumptious buzzards, each of them voicing a multilingual directive to cease flight. Mihail wondered if they were strong enough to hold his weight. Could he grab one and have it fly him over to the shipping container? Probably not. Heavily battered in appearance, their working parts were likely many-times recycled. He imagined one of them exploding internally, coughing out plumes of black soot, and spiralling down with him holding onto it like a fool.

Mihail gripped the wooden guardrail, lifted himself onto it, stood at half his height, and looked out over a gap that seemed a thousand turbans long. The distance between here and the ground was even greater.

The flimsy railing moved back and forth like a tightrope with an indeterminate centre of gravity. Mihail was terrified that, if he jumped, the transferal of his weight to the guardrail would snap the wood and he'd plunge like a deluded super hero.

'I don't think I can make it, Charles.'

'You can, buddy. But you have to believe you can.'

'Oh don't serve me *that*!'

'Just jump, buddy. Jump!'

'I'm just going to... I'm just going to... *jump*!!!!'

Mihail jumped off the guardrail, his spring feeling so devoid of gusto that he was certain he'd be victimised by gravity. But instead of plummeting, he somehow sailed. He landed with a heavy *cong* right on the edge of the shipping container, and would have fallen backwards had Charles not lunged forward and grabbed the shoulder of his robe.

'Good work, buddy! Now let's go!'

The drones chased them across the iron rooftops, which *conged* every time their feet landed. Trap doors opened; more irate residents peered out. One of them was a disfigured woman who was obviously the victim of a declined-marriage acid-attack. The quartet made use of her appearance (as in entrance) by bustling through her trap door.

Barging through the woman's cramped living room and through her front door, they bashed into a pair of virtue-promoting vice-preventers about to conduct an inspection. The portly men were shocked, fell back, made a pair of *congs*, and speedily broke out their wooden rulers (which were usually reserved for measuring the distance between unmarried men and women [and for chastising those who failed to employ the correct amount of distance]). Battering all three Musvestites and the short brown man chaperoning them, the *veepee-veepees* – as they were slanderously known – chased them down a corridor so tight that they all had to shuffle sideways as they *conged* their way through it.

Several corners later the six of them broke through into a stuffy room stuffed with stuffing and children. These countless exhausted juveniles were hard at work using sewing machines to make teddy bears for export.

'Sorry to interrupt!' shouted Mihail, as he rebounded – *cong* – off a wall, and grabbed clumps of stuffing to throw at the veepee-veepees, who expertly swatted it away with their wooden rulers. 'Ignore us; focus on your productivity! KPIs, children!'

Exiting the sweatshop and colliding with another corridor – *cong* – they ricocheted out of it and emerged into a steep canyon of shipping containers, many raggedly gouged open to become shopfronts. The balconies and bridges skirting and spanning the chasm were made of reconstituted wooden pallets. Zin Kadeshians swarmed across them, dispersing through an emporium whose vast ceiling was a canopy of faded corrugated plastic. At the bottom of it all was a muddy channel of water, upholding a string of shipping containers being rolled across floating steel drums. Inside the containers were sun-bleached packages that looked like bags of fertiliser. Men unloading them were doing so under the watchful gaze of men with machine guns. These international food donations were the property of the Zin Kadeshi government, and would either be hoarded, or sold at a premium.

They shook off the veepee-veepees when darting into a meaty forest of dangling pig corpses. For good measure, Mihail grabbed the gory body of a still-living frog that had been stripped of its skin and pelted it at them.

Descending metal panels welded between containers led them deeper into a foreboding maze of iron alleyways. Decorative electrical bulbs illuminated shadowy doorways. Although most of the prostitutes standing inside them appeared to be women, the majority were actually men, men who'd undergone reconstructive surgery in order to command a higher price. The feeding of one's family can require certain sacrifices. For this reason, Mihail respectfully dipped his keffiyeh as he hurried past.

At one point they turned a corner and stumbled over a crippled beggar aged about ten. A representative hurried forward, accused them of injuring the poor boy, and demanded compensation for the damage. The outraged intervener of course didn't mention that he was the one who'd crippled the boy – having maimed him as a baby so that he'd grow up to produce a better rate of alms. The man was a beggar's agent, who of course received a 100 percent commission. In spite of this entrepreneur's passionate speech, Mihail waggled a knowing finger and continued on.

Bringing out his phone, Mihail invoked a three-dimensional imbroglio of a map that was further complicated by stacking advertisements. Thanks to practice he was able to see through it all. He determined their position and located the nearest gondola station.

Leading the way down corridors that made them feel like cave explorers, he brought them to a hallway that rumbled as if veiling a great machine. A crowd lodged inside it jabbered in many languages. Up ahead, chunks of the crowd were scooped away whenever a whooshing steel object swept into view.

When they arrived at the front of the line, a metal bench swept beneath them, slapped their legs out from under them, and lifted them off their feet. It swung around a corner and – *whoosh* – carried them out over an inglorious spread of grime and shoddiness: a jagged realm of streets and avenues that resembled cracks in dried mud.

The gondola was the city's most effective means of transportation through high-density areas. The only problem was, sometimes the cables snapped and all the passengers plummeted. The chairs approaching them appeared liable to produce that outcome. Most were overloaded and pulling heavily on the cable.

Despite the potential danger, the gondola ride was a soothing intermission. Its gentle lolling almost had them yawning as they looked out across neighbourhoods, some of them bulging with concrete fortifications. These bland tasteless mansions were indicative of how commerce, corruption, or a combination, had crowned its kings.

'Hey buddy,' said Charles. 'I know I should not laugh, but it is yes very funny. When the ticket inspector saw the face of that one, do you know what he said? He said, *That is one ugly woman.*'

Charles and Mihail began laughing – so hard that the Originals joined them. The gondola began to sway. And perhaps that was why a drone dropped out of the sky and focused its beady bulb directly onto them.

All four men reacted instantly. Each lunged in a particular direction, but checked their respective impulse and stayed seated.

'Oh buddy. What are we going to do? Now the police will be waiting for us at the other end. I do not want to go to a Zin Kadeshi gaol. I have heard too many stories.'

Beneath their gondola swept another gondola, travelling crosswise to their own. Seeing this, and noting more of these transecting cables, Mihail considered leaping onto a passing chair beneath. But how would that aid their plight? The drone would just follow them to the new gondola.

They were too high up to jump to anywhere safely – unless perhaps they leapt onto one of the pylons as they passed it. But again, the drone would just follow them. By now it had already scanned their faces; and by the time they reached the ground it would have so many reinforcements buzzing around that escape would be impossible – even if they split up.

'It shall not end here, Charles,' said Mihail, with determination. 'The plan I have is historical. This rubbish will become a masterpiece.'

By *rubbish* he was referring to their circumstances, which did yes appear overwhelming and inescapable. But there *had* to be a pathway to salvation. There always is.

And there it was. Or at least, there it *might* be. Would it be close enough to leap to? The looming tower, called a Paddy Stack, was a structure that looked like fifty or so gigantic lily pads skewered by vertical poles. It was at least fifty metres high, and their cable travelled directly over it.

Mihail lifted the gondola's bar and said, 'I believe we can make it, Charles.'

'Oh buddy.' There was a note panic in the African's voice. 'I do not know if that is wise. They are not very strong.'

'But there's water at the bottom, Charles. They catch it and re-use it. Besides: Is there any other option?'

'I do not think there is,' said Charles, glumly.

'Then let's tell our friends we're going to... jump.'

'We should also maybe tell them,' said Charles, 'that Zin Kadeshi hospitals are terribly under-professional, under-staffed, and under-supplied.'

'Children in their country don't even *have* hospitals, Charles.'

' – And that a broken bone,' continued Charles, 'will be left to heal itself.'

'I think they'll be grateful just to be looking at a ceiling.'

'I hope they also know,' said Charles, as the gondola carried them almost directly above the Paddy Stack, 'that Zin Kadeshi ambulances are very very famous for, how you say, kidnapping people and stealing their body pieces.'

'I believe it's called harvesting organs, Charles,' said Mihail, with burgeoning hysteria. 'And yes it's a risk. But when is life in Zin Kadesh ever NOT A RISK?!!!'

Mihail dropped off the gondola and plunged toward the top rice field. It tore the moment he struck it. Level after level ripped apart as he rolled one way then another, fortunately always missing the wooden scaffolding that allowed workers to tend the fields. Those workers, prone on skateboards, gawked in disbelief as Mihail crashed through their livelihoods. The cumulative resistance of the thick, stringy, muddy membranes so effectively slowed him down that by the time he reached the bottom of the Paddy Stack he gently *plopped* into the water catchment beneath.

An explosion shortly followed. It was Charles hitting the water, of course with no membranous rice fields to slow his fall. The Originals were luckier: they'd landed on a section of material that Mihail hadn't destroyed, and were so aided by the intermittent resistance that they almost didn't break through the final layer. It distended then pierced, and the pair dropped through as if vertically birthed.

There was much laughter from the Chaperone and the Chaperoned as they swam for the exit. It greatly contrasted with the swearing and curses coming from the tenders of the rice fields. Mihail felt badly for them, what with how their rate of pay was probably only four cents an hour.

Weary workers in conical hats tried to accost them, but the quartet was so charged with adrenaline that its members ducked, dodged, darted, and laughed their heads off as they headed for the entrance. The compound's barbed wire gate opened as they approached it, probably because their confident stride suggested authority.

The street outside was teeming with home-made motorbikes, rusty cycling contraptions, and cow patties. Livestock had free reign in this part of the city – but for how long, was the question. "Balance brawls" were a common occurrence between those who regarded cows as sacred and those who didn't. One was taking place right now. Zin Kadeshians of all creeds had been dragged into its epicentre. They were biffing and throwing each other around – a ravenous mass of bodies that circulated like a storm cloud.

A shirtless man on a shabby scooter braked in front of the brawl, propped his bike on its kickstand, screamed like a warrior of old, and flung himself into the fray. The engine of his scooter was still running. By happenstance (or maybe something more) the bike had a wooden platform at the back of it, ideal for passengers. The owner didn't even notice as three drenched Musvestites and a soggy chaperone clambered onto his scooter and puttered away. He had two different men by their beards and was conking their heads together.

Deftly avoiding cow patties (which, when smeared, frequently preceded a crashed vehicle), Mihail steered through lawless traffic that seemed to lurch at them from all angles. Pedestrians waded through the midst of it, never making eye contact with drivers or riders, and miraculously making it to the other side.

The frenetic traffic slowed almost to a sedate crawl. It wasn't long before Mihail glimpsed the reason why. Up ahead was a roadblock, manned by policemen wearing military grade body armour. Parked behind them were vehicles that looked like diamond-encased quad-bikes. These glassy miniature tanks each had a driver and a gunner.

'We have a challenge, Charles. 'I think I might just try to discreetly steer us in another direction.'

Mihail's tack through the congestion sparked an increase of honks, beeps and swearing. He did his best to be overtly apologetic. Naturally, this admission of wrongdoing and the begging of forgiveness was pounced upon. The honking, beeping and swearing intensified.

His worst fear materialised when a drone appeared, bobbing overhead like a dead bug in water. The hideous machine rotated, pitched toward them, and intoned, 'Stop in the Name of the Law.'

'The Law is the last thing I'm going to stop for!' shouted Mihail, pulling back on the throttle, and bouncing the scooter up onto the footpath. He veered around and accelerated away from roadblock. Looking in one of the bike's rear-view mirrors, he saw the exact moment the tanks began chasing. Two of them lunged forward and ploughed through the traffic as if it was nothing but a field of mannequins. A sandalled pedestrian went flipping off the side of one tank and beneath the chunky tyres of another. Doubtless there would be no consequences for these "public servants." In Zin Kadesh, the Law was above the law.

A man toting a wheelbarrow filled with plastic water bottles lost his balance when the whining scooter shot past him. The bottles hit the ground, split open, and he started crying. Another man, this one trolleying a wire cage bulging with tarantulas, abandoned his wares and dove for safety. Mihail swerved, but the bike's rear hit the cage. Its latch flew open, and a million high-protein insects flurried with excitement – as did Mihail, who almost let go of the handle bars to slap himself clean. If any spiders had made the transfer to his person, he'd simply have to endure it. Gritting his teeth, keeping the throttle all the way back, he leaned into a turn that split apart a goat herd, and motored up a pedestrian ramp made of particle board and bamboo struts.

And not a moment too soon! The minute they left the crowded street there was an explosion, followed quickly by more explosions. The police tanks had entered the neighbourhood-kingdom of a local warlord. His child soldiers had emerged with machine guns and rocket launchers, and were blasting away at the "pork mothers." The crystal carapaces quickly shattered, the policemen were yanked out of their vehicles and hacked apart with machetes. The gleeful ghetto symphony reached a bombastic height when an eleven-year-old started throwing out coin-sized land mines like they were lollies. The civilians who trod on them exploded into pink mist, their meaty limbs raining down like gifts from heaven.

Mihail could see all this from the ramp, whose succeeding diagonal paths afforded a view of the entire street. In spite of the chaos and the carnage, the drone was still with them. In fact it was joined by several colleagues. Like spiders catching updrafts they ascended in pursuit. Mihail wished the scooter had a bigger engine. It so struggled with the uphill gradient that it was barely overtaking a convoy of shopping trolleys towed by a golf cart. The armed teenagers escorting the train chuckled as the scooter inched past them.

Finally they made it to the top of the ramp, where they looked out across a never-ending neighbourhood of aged emergency tents. The smudgy fabric domes were accessible by wooden scaffolds resting on a choppy ocean of corrugated iron and plastic tarp. Along these planks trudged pilgrims in untold numbers, sometimes disappearing when their path bottomed out from beneath them. Setting out across the same terrain was a risk, but an unavoidable one. The vulturous drones were right behind them.

Mihail gunned the engine and steered over wooden planks wired together end to end. He could feel them undulating underneath as though floating on water. Every time his tyres crossed from one plank to another there was a *badoonk badoonk* noise. It was a welcome relief from the bovine screams coming from the nearby abbatower. Ironically (what with the sacred cows nearby) they were in a suburb that had grown around a huge steel monolith famed for its torturous methods of butchery.

A wrong turn took them through the centre of a rooftop wedding ceremony. The father of the seven-year-old bride was positively incensed. He took off a sandal and ditched it, leading others to do the same. Fortunately, the scooter was gone before anybody realised there were three Musvestites perched on the back of it.

Some of the drones overtook them, while others yawed, dropped, and pinwheeled to various places alongside them. Thankfully, they were approaching an off-ramp – identical to the on-ramp they'd just made use of. Un-thankfully, there was a dray full of melons lodged against the corner of its entrance. The man pulling it had miscalculated his turn and gotten stuck. No one was helping him; passersby were more squeezersby. Mihail aimed to join them. *Badoonk badoonk, badoonk badoonk, badoonk badoonk. Meep meep meeeeeeppp!!* shrilled his horn. Nobody listened, because everyone honked at everyone in Zin Kadesh. It was cultural.

Mihail braked, waggled the handlebars, and inserted the bike through the gap. A piping, zipping noise slashed past his ear, and a black dart thudded into a melon. Vibrating like an arrow in a target, it signified a new phase of the chase. The authorities were firing at them, but not with their usual bullets or plumes of flame – with tranquillisers! Evidently they'd identified the Original Australians, and were actively trying to avoid any international incidents.

Charles grabbed hold of a melon and lobbed it at one of the drones. It was a direct hit! The floating machine rocked backward then shook like a recovering boxer. Charles was about throw another, when the same noise as before whipped through the air, and the burqa'd Original to his left slumped over. The exact same process repeated, this time with the Original to his right. The drone responsible rotated and placed its beady lens on Charles. Its dart-shooting barrel folded up into its underside. Out came a small turbine gun.

Charles screamed and ditched the melon, which hit the drone so hard that it (the melon) splattered. By this point Mihail had brought the scooter all the way around the dray. He revved the throttle and off they went, turning, several slopes down, into a corridor that pedestrians were funnelling through. Charles was hanging on to the floppy Originals, trying desperately to prevent their falling off. Every corner had been a gravity-induced nightmare. Now, in a dark and dingy passageway clogged with Zin Kadeshians, gravity was assailing him not from the sides but from above and beneath. Every time they rode over a lump they soared off the bench and crashed back onto it.

Motorbikes weren't typically appropriate for tight bustling corridors. The irritated pedestrians made this known. Mihail came to a cross-corridor and was meant to give way, but he maintained speed and – *bang* – collided with a cartful of plastic bottles, towed by a man on a lanky tricycle. The cart flipped over and empty bottles sprayed everywhere. People lunging to snatch them held them up as if they were treasures. Mihail, motoring onward, watched them scramble for the bottles, and suddenly had an idea.

'Charles!' he shouted. 'Can you access your phone?'

'No buddy! I am trying for them not to fall off!'

'We need a map!' said Mihail. 'We need to find a highway!'

A drone was right behind them, just below the ceiling and planing over the heads of the crowd. It looked like a flying version of one of the tarantulas that Mihail imagined he could still feel crawling across his skin. He was watching the drone in a rear view mirror, wondering why it wasn't shooting.

The further they zoomed down the corridor, the darker and less populated it became. Ominous-looking symbols appeared on the walls. Mihail recognised them and slowed to a stop, in spite of the drone just behind him. In fact, the drone also halted, seemingly just as worried. Mihail knew why. If it wanted to ensure the lives of these two Originals, it had a paltry chance of doing it in this place.

'Buddy? Why have you stopped?'

'I'm just going to turn around and...' Mihail trailed off into silence.

Ahead of them, stepping into a dim pool of flickering fluorescent light, were three shirtless men, their faces and bodies tattooed with the same insignia graffitied on the walls. Protruding from their waistbands were the handles of pistols. The middle gangster gave a smile that was half enamel and half gold. Putting a cigarette to his lips, he took a deep and languorous puff. Its tip glowed like a pebble mined from hell.

Mihail nervously said, 'Uh, would you gentlemen mind helping us against the law?'

The three men looked at one another... and burst out laughing. The sound of it was disturbing.

'Certainly,' said the middle gangster, his eyes gleaming. 'We will help you. Just come with us. Down here, this way.'

Following the men down a dark passage was the last thing Mihail wanted to do, but a three-point turn in a space this wide was totally inconceivable. His eyes flicked down to the scooter's oval dash. Next to its speedometer was something that flicked his heart with hope. It was an *R* – presumably for *reverse*.

'Lead the way,' said Mihail, with a generous gesture.

'Oh no no no, please please,' said the middle gangster, stepping aside to make way. 'After you.'

Mihail shifted the gear stick of the idling scooter. The *R* symbol glowed red. Hopefully it *did* stand for reverse. If something else happened he'd be severely embarrassed. Twisting the throttle, he waited anxiously for it to bite, and the moment it did – *yoooom* – the scooter launched backwards.

Blazing flares of gunfire exploded through the corridor, coming mostly from the drone! The gangsters barely had time to reach for their weapons. But bursting out of doorways came more gangsters, wielding shotguns and machine guns, whose buckshot and bullets straightaway ripped through the walls, ceiling and floor. The drone jiggled around as it was pummelled, and then – *woooooooooffffff* – it triggered a thick plume of flame that engulfed the gangsters.

All of this Mihail saw as he reversed with iron wrists, terrified that the slightest wobble would topple them. The first cross-corridor he motored past, he braked, put the bike in normal gear, then accelerated forward and turned down it.

The subterranean-seeming hallway was filled more gangsters, launching out of doorways with weapons in hand. They sprinted in the direction of the furore, so intently that the scooter speeding through their midst was practically invisible to them. The sound of gunfire hammered through the corridor, followed by a large explosion. No doubt the gang's drug lab had just caught on fire.

When the entire building finally exploded, its fiery splintery gust knocked over a family of fifteen that was loaded onto the one motorbike. Mihail and the others whizzed past them, fortunate that the blast hit them from behind as opposed to the side. Airborne for a good long moment, they landed in a straight line and continued on, Charles still clinging to the Originals.

The remaining drones hadn't forgotten about them. The whining mosquitoes descended from all angles, clinging to the quartet like flies on –

'Oh no,' said Charles. 'Oh no. I cannot hold him.'

One of the Originals had rolled off Charles' lap and was hanging off the back of the bike. Charles struggled valiantly to hang onto him, but the young Musvestite was too heavy. He fell, hit the bitumen, rolled, and lay still – a heap of black fabric on the street. Two of the drones stopped chasing and lingered at his side. At least he would be safe.

'Should we give them the other one as well, buddy? Maybe they will stop chasing us, yes?'

'We need him, Charles. Without him, all we'll be is yet another pair of rounded-up border-breachers!'

'I am looking forward to hearing your plan, buddy!'

'I'm looking forward to finishing it!'

A steel ramp hemmed by squirls of barbed wire did a wide spiral up to a concrete highway, a highway that stretched out over slums like a crowd-surfing tape worm. The rolling cityscape swelled with mounds and valleys that could make a traveller seasick. Mihail paid it no attention: his eyes were locked on the two lanes of traffic he was motoring between, one flowing with him, the other toward him. He didn't need a map now that he was on an elevated road. He knew exactly where he was going.

The drones formed a solid squadron – a hovering escort that trailed them on their serpentine path until finally Mihail pulled over to the side of the road. He hopped off the seat, not bothering with the kickstand, hurried around to the back of the scooter, and helped Charles hold onto the Original as the bike fell away from them and clattered onto the ground. They bustled the unconscious Original over to the guardrail, laid him flat upon it, and looked over at a raging river of traffic that flowed beneath their road.

'Buddy. I do not understand.'

'We're going to jump, Charles. And we're taking this person with us.'

'Wh... I *still* do not understand.'

'Just trust me, Charles. It's the second best idea I've had today.'

The drones all had their weapons out – only they couldn't shoot because if Charles and Mihail let go of their hostage he would probably fall and be killed.

'We shouldn't be waiting too long,' said Mihail. 'They're always on this highway, because of how much it slopes. There was a major sinkhole a few suburbs away. They still haven't done anything about it. Probably never will.'

Brushing his keffiyeh out of his eyes, he gazed into the distance, thinking for a moment that he'd seen one. He was wrong. But less than a minute later, he was right. Pointing at the traffic spilling over the furthest visible point of the highway, he said, 'There, Charles. Salvation.'

The wheeled vehicle looked like a cow-catcher made out of wire. This light-weight frame had twelve skinny brown men who were pedalling to keep it going, and towed a long, open-top trailer made of chicken wire. Inside the trailer were thousands of colourful bottles. Whether those bottles were glass or plastic was an issue of great importance, what with Mihail's intention to leap down onto them.

'Oh buddy. *Is* this a good idea?'

'I probably shouldn't answer that, Charles. Just... just make sure to aim properly.'

Mihail had the Original by the legs, Charles had him by the shoulders. Both climbed over the guardrail and watched the approaching semi-cycler. Gauging when to jump was an excruciating decision. Too early and *splat*. Too late and *splat*.

'Alright buddy, let us hope for the best.'

'I agree, Charles. Let's do that, and let's do it... Not yet... Not yet... Not yet... NOW!'

They stepped off the elevated highway and dragged the Original with them, toward hard merciless bitumen that expanded beneath them, and a vicious torrent of machinery that would squash them like pilgrims. A cow in a passing rickshaw made a drawn-out insulting noise. But the joke was on it, because

Charles, Mihail, and the unconscious Original, were summarily delivered from the clutch of death. A rectangle of colourful bubbles swept beneath them at the perfect moment and – *booosh* – they landed in a mobile pool of empty plastic bottles. They slipped beneath the surface and disappeared in a skittling sea of pliable plastic.

'Hahaaaa!' shouted Charles, rustling amid the bottles. 'Buddy! I thought we were going to die!'

'So did I, Charles! It seems our sleeping friend is a good luck charm! There's no *way* those drones can keep up with us.'

'Hopefully when we stop the police will not be waiting.'

'We'll have abandoned ship long before then, Charles. (Provided our friend wakes up). This is actually quite ideal: it gives me time to consider all the details of my plan.'

'You are confident with it, yes?'

'What with how everything else has worked in our favour, yes, Charles, I am. Very confident. But I have to admit, it will be dangerous. And for it to be effective, we'll have to be...' He didn't want to say it... 'injured.'

'Injured, buddy? Very, how you say, badly?'

'The badder the better, I'm afraid. But look at it this way, Charles. If we execute this idea of mine well enough, never again will we have to call ourselves Zin Kadeshians.'

XVII

It was three o'clock in the morning, at a place where a monstrous pile of garbage had so overwhelmed the Zin Kadeshi border fence that that part of it was flat to the ground and buried beneath a talus of rotting junk. Descending the rubbish were fifteen or so children, performing a skilful and funny-to-watch task: They were laying wooden planks on the rubbish, balancing a scooter on top, and escorting the scooter down the slope – a child on either side of the handle bars to apply the brakes, and a child at the back to provide stability. Three scooters required three units of plank-layers and support kids. Behind them trudged Charles, Mihail, and the Musvestite Original, each carrying different items.

These children were orphans who lived within this vast and mountainous garbage dump. Commonly regarded as innately inferior and thus unworthy of help, they fossicked for food to eat or items to sell, and had agreed to help these strangers in exchange for their transaction cards. Charles and Mihail had shown them how much money was in their respective accounts, and said the children could have all of it – on conditions they must seriously agree to. The first was: Whenever they accessed the money, they should run from that location as fast as possible, for fear of being caught by the police. The second was: they should always divide the money equally. The third was: No sugary products were to be bought with the money. Mihail was adamant about this, telling them that tooth rot out here, without access to a dentist, would be horrendous to endure. 'In fact look, I don't want to tell you how to spend your money, but the services of a dentist would be very beneficial. You can't sit around waiting for COAU aid-workers to do the yearly rounds.'

The kids deposited the scooters on Contemporary Australian soil. Charles and Mihail handed over their transaction cards, extracting from the orphans yet another promise to adhere to the conditions. One boy had flattened plastic bottles for shoes. He was scrawny, as they all were, and smiled brilliantly when showing Charles' card to his sister. She was six months old.

The scooters and everything loaded on them had been appropriated from an Expansionist depot – everything save for the large plastic panels which had been 3d printed by a good (and trustworthy) friend of Mihail's. The panels were propped on the back of the scooters and leaned against their riders. The orphans draped a swathe of textured tarpaulin over each man and his bike. Hopefully this would conceal them from satellites and helicopters. From above they would blend in with the sand.

The three refugees ignited their bikes and wheeled around. After a final goodbye to the waving orphans, they puttered away into the desert.

Mihail had one eye on the rocky ground ahead, and one eye on a rear-view mirror. He watched his city recede into the darkness, wondering if he'd ever get to see it again. Emotions are a funny thing, he mused. Here he was finally escaping the country he had for so long criticised, and now he just wanted to turn around, go back to it and never leave it. How strange.

The Original, who had had some riding practice several hours earlier, was already as good as Charles and Mihail. Not once did he lose his balance, and he was wise enough not to let excitement tamper with his rate of speed. He was riding in the middle of the trio, with Mihail in front and Charles behind. He had been quite distraught when learning his friend was no longer with them. Mihail had finally calmed him by convincing him (via an electronic translator) that they would be reunited in the place they were going to.

After forty-five minutes of riding through the desert with their lights off, they arrived at the Longreaching Highway. Hefty concrete pillars kept it elevated ten metres above the ground. In the darkness they were like soldiers, or megaliths, immovable and innumerable. The road was raised for the chief purpose of preserving wildlife.

Propping their scooters on their kickstands, they began assembling the components of what they had decided should be called the Freedom Mobile. Its inner framework was a wooden construction that looked like an elongated *pi* symbol. Its exterior was made of four plastic stencils that they added shape to by applying heat in marked places. These plastic quarters snapped together, and became the lightweight carapace of a shiny yellow hatchback car.

A nifty device called a rigidifying roll-up ladder gave them access to the high-up highway. Once there, they used a motor-winch to lift the three bikes, and then the car shell and wooden chassis, up onto the road.

The chassis clamped onto the scooters, connecting them in a trio whereby there were two bikes at the front and one at the back. When the men climbed onto the bikes (Mihail and Charles at the front, the Original at the back) they lifted the car shell up and over themselves, and tied it to their scooters so it wouldn't fly away. Charles and Mihail looked at each other and nodded, both impressed. This low-cost means of effecting a status symbol veiled quite nicely the illegality of scooters on a highway.

Their engines came to life and they twisted their throttles in unison. The Freedom Mobile began whirring down the Longreaching Highway.

In not long they had picked up speed, but not nearly enough to be satisfying. In a country this vast they had neither the time nor the fuel to make it to anywhere civilised. But this reality had been anticipated and accounted for.

Behind them, coming steadily up the highway, was a vehicle that shortly revealed itself to be a 4-wheel-drive towing a caravan. Mihail, seated on the right, covered his face as the vehicle overtook them. He need not have worried. The driver and passenger, both grey-haired, were deeply engrossed in video games.

The moment the caravan finished passing them, they swerved the Freedom Mobile in behind it. Charles reached through the space where the windshield should have been, and flung a length of rope that uncoiled and lassoed around the caravan's towball. The lasso cinched closed, and a rappelling device attached to the front of the wooden chassis gradually released the rope so that sudden tension didn't tear the front off the car.

'Ha,' said Charles. 'I did not think that was going to work. Congratulations to us, yes?'

Two hours later, when the sun was a molten nub on the horizon, the rope slackened, and a light collision with the caravan awakened Charles from a shallow doze.

'Ah! Refugee camp,' he said, looking around in fear until he gained his bearings.

Ahead of them, a slight bend in the highway allowed them to see beyond the caravan. They were heading for a gleaming building that looked like a bloated silver photo frame. The highway passed through it. This was a border checkpoint.

Applying the brakes to avoid further collisions with the caravan as it continued to slow, they joined a queue waiting to be admitted past the checkpoint. When the 4-wheel-drive reached the front of the line, they disconnected from its caravan, and eagerly watched it proceed.

The moment the caravan crossed the borderline, out of the road sprang a wall of crisscrossing steel bars – like a net made of lengthy switchblades. The checkpoint was immediately more intimidating. Nodding with resolve, Mihail gave the signal, and all three of them accelerated.

The checkpoint was a looming structure seemingly at the end of a slippery treadmill. But finally they were beneath its bureaucratic shadow, idling next to a uniformed man in a glass booth.

'Welcome to checkpoint S, State 3, COAU,' said the bored-looking border patrolman. 'Please present for retinal scanning by looking to one's right. If you have any fruit or vegetables please declare them.'

'Uh, we do have something to declare,' said Mihail, 'though it's not a fruit or vegetable – or flora or fauna, heh heh. Have you heard of the Original Australian that hasn't yet been apprehended? Well, that's him in the back; and I, Sayeed Mihail, along with my colleague Charles Gaco, hereby inform you, that if you do not let us past this checkpoint, we will ensure that the explosives strapped to the body of this Original Australian will be detonated. As a result, he will be blown all the way back to his beloved Dreamtime, and it will be entirely your fault.'

The patrolman turned and looked closely at... at a burqa'd woman on the backseat of a scooter. His eyes scanned the rest of the vehicle, and then there was a *tk* sound as he turned off his intercom. Obviously conferring with a supervisor, there was another *tk* noise, and he asked, 'Would you mind please lowering the contraband item on the lady's face?'

Mihail gestured for the Original to lower his veil. When that happened, the skepticism slid off the patrolman's face, and he looked at Mihail with bulging eyes.

'I understand your country has a no negotiation policy with terrorists,' said Mihail. 'I think this situation might call for an exception.'

Tk. And a few moments later another man stepped into the booth. After conferring with the patrolman, the supervisor leaned forward and began speaking, but couldn't be heard because the intercom was off. There was a *tk* (thanks to the quiet patrolman) and the supervisor finished saying, 'Aborigine?'

'That is correct,' said Mihail. 'However I don't think they like being called that. As I was saying to your associate: we want that gate opened, and we want it opened now, otherwise we will activate the explosives strapped to the person of this Original Australian– person. I'm sure you've performed a scan of this vehicle, and found distinct traces of charcoal, sulphur, and potassium nitrate.

I think you might just have a duty of care to believe that we are serious.'

The bulge beneath the Original's dress wasn't in fact an explosive device, but rather an animal-skin carry-bag he was adamant not to part with.

Attempting to be a man of both charm and reason, the supervisor said, 'How 'bout we pull over into one of the waiting bays, so the rest of the traffic can keep moving?'

Mihail shook his head.

A *tk* preceded a silent conversation between the two bureaucrats. Another *tk* went before the question, 'How do we know you're not just gonna blow up that Aborigine the moment you cross the border?'

Mihail, prepared for that question, puffed up indignantly, as planned, and pronounced, 'How *dare* you! What an *ignorant* generalisation! Such offensiveness is on par with your country's reprehensible *Wear a Burqa Grab a Child and Drag Them into a Public Toilet Day*! Your lack of sensitivity is so outrageous, I can easily see how somebody *would* be marginalised into thinking, It is time – to detonate – the Original – Australian! Ya-la-la-la-la-la-la-la-la-la!'

The last utterance was a waggle-tongued war cry intended to confuse. And it worked! The patrolman and the supervisor, both pale and apologising furiously, bumped heads as they scrambled to find the right button. Finally they did, and the bladed border fence retracted into the ground.

'Thank you, gentlemen, said Mihail, with marked poise. 'Your country owes you a debt of gratitude.' He and the two others pulled back on their throttles and whirred away from the booth. The two men inside it stared after the odd vehicle. The Original Australian inside it was peering back at them intently.

The Freedom Mobile motored past the borderline, and continued down an open stretch of highway that was as good to the Zin Kadeshians as a pot of pure untaxable gold. Within minutes they were being tailed by four border patrol cars: white armoured vehicles that gave them plenty of space. The border-breachers learned the reason for the latitude by way of Mihail's phone, which was taped to his scooter's dash and tuned to the relevant frequency. 'Be advised,' said a bureaucratic voice, 'the order of action is to hold back and wait for a specialised unit. I repeat, the order of action is to hold back and wait for a specialised unit.

In the blue sky above the yellow hatchback there appeared a glinting speck, a speck that raced closer till it became a glassy missile, a missile that disintegrated into thousands of orbs, each the size of a golf ball. They filtered down, surrounded the situation, and began recording it from a multitude of angles. These droplet-looking machines were called media pods, and they were now broadcasting this event all around the planet. Mihail confirmed it by reaching for his phone. He accessed a news channel and straightaway found an image of the Freedom Mobile.

'I believe,' said Mihail, 'this is what is known as showtime.'

Taking off a backpack he'd been wearing, he reached inside it and produced a toy baby, life-sized and swaddled in a white cloth. He handed it to Charles then produced an identical baby for himself.

The media coverage was showing audience reactions to the "hostage crisis at the COAU border." Solemn faces from all over the world were watching intently (probably to spot themselves on the bottom of their screens). Mihail felt slightly giddy when thinking that soon he would be among them – only blown up far larger, and with a much bigger part to play.

The media pods zoomed in closer on the boxy yellow hatchback. Viewers were surprised when the car did a slow backflip and landed on its roof, revealing itself not to be a genuine hatchback, but a fake car that had been concealing three men on scooters. Two of them were clutching babies, while the third was smeared in white body paint and wearing a red loincloth. People gasped when realising: it was the missing Original Australian.

The three men on scooters revved their engines and took off down the highway. From out the back of their bikes unfurled home-made banners, reading, *www.zkplight.com.umcau.* This website, which Mihail had put together yesterday afternoon, showcased photographs and footage of Zin Kadeshian hardships, and featured a short video (filmed at the garbage dump) that highlighted some of the UMCAU's many social problems. Appealing for people to reach into their hearts and consider the ills of others, he asked if some out there in the world might help generate groundswell, for a movement that would engender further movement, namely the outward expansion of the UMCAU's territory. 'Of course we realise we're asking a lot. But we also understand the commonalities that bridge the gap between us. It's *those* things I ask you to consider. As you go about your daily lives, I hope you will remember that There But for the Grace of Blind Good Fortune... Go I. Moreover, I hope you follow the link that leads to our petition. We intend to give it the Contemporary Australian government, in the hope that those in positions of power will make a decision that recognises the plight of the far less fortunate.'

Viewers with short attention spans followed the link before the video finished, signed their names to the petition, returned to the media coverage, and had no idea, because they hadn't completed Mihail's appeal, that the babies being held up by two of the scooter riders, were in fact *toy* babies, symbolic of generations yet to be. On the graphs charting audience comments, a blade-shaped mountain spiked into being, signifying concern for the two babies. It was closely followed by a tiny flick of a triangle: the amount of people clarifying that those babies were actually plastic.

Mihail was roaring down the highway, holding up the swaddled baby in what he felt must surely be an iconic image. Not noticing that the media pods had slightly retreated, he was startled when a glass box suddenly *whooshed* past him. Big enough to easily fit two scooters and their riders inside it, the glass box was attached to a hydraulic arm extruding from a helicopter.

'All units be advised,' said the bureaucratic voice emanating from Mihail's phone, 'the specialised unit has arrived. The apprehension of the Original Australian will now commence. The order of action is to continue proceeding with caution, and do not intervene.'

The glass box hovered above the Original Australian. Had he not looked up, seen it coming, and swerved, it would have stamped down and trapped him like a bug in a jar. Instead, the box scraped the road and came around for another attempt. Again the Original evaded it. He was fast. Very fast. He had the reflexes of... of an Original Australian.

Charles was zigzagging across the road, ably performing according to Mihail's instructions. His baby was high for the media pods to see. He shook it as if to say *Look*. The audience didn't like that. Seismic spikes appeared above symbols representing emotions like *dissatisfaction, pity,* and *outrage.* Intellectuals appearing in pop up boxes were saying that the handling of this situation on the Longreaching Highway would no doubt plague the current government for many years to come. They were likely correct, what with how the helicopter swung its glass box at the Original, but missed him, clobbered Charles, and sent the African veering toward the guardrail. Charles crashed into the barrier and flipped over the top of it. Mihail, watching on his phone, saw Charles fall ten long metres before slamming onto scrubland. Mihail was shocked, even though everything was going to plan. Gripping his handlebars tightly, knowing that his own plunge over the side was imminent, he throttled forward with resolve, and again held up his toy baby for the wider world to see.

The glass box swung left and right like a pendulum, ignoring Mihail and aiming for the Original, who adeptly dodged it by braking and swerving. Mihail ducked and the crystal container swished over his head. He braked and it swept past his front wheel. The box wobbled alongside him, lifted, and grew larger in his field of vision till there was nothing in the world but glass. A bump on the side of his bike sent him motoring toward the guardrail. He could have corrected his course, but why prolong the inevitable/necessary?

Mihail crashed into the guardrail; his scooter bucked and threw him off its seat. Over the railing he flipped, the sky and the ground repeatedly trading places. Because in one hand he clutched the toy baby, and in the other hand his phone, he looked like a person taking a selfie with their child, oblivious to the fact that they were somersaulting toward a potentially fatal outcome. He was concentrating on the live footage of his own falling self, which flattened out into a belly flop as it plunged.

During his last few metres of free-fall, Mihail looked away from his phone, and saw rocky ground rushing up to meet him. He cringed, and when he awoke, he heard a voice saying that there was a lot of controversy over the fact that this person – Sayeed Mihail – had, on impact, used a baby to shield his own face. Said baby was lying on the dirt, next to the prattling phone. Even though the effort sent flares of agony through his body, Mihail crawled over to his phone, angled it so he could see it properly, and continued watching the media coverage, keenly interested in how many viewers he had.

The Original Australian in the body paint and red loincloth was still evading capture. The glass box was coming at him from all angles, but he weaved on his scooter and easily avoided it. That is, until the box tried to preempt his location, and perfectly positioned itself in a place where the Original drove straight into it.

There was a multinational gasp when the Original, apparently stunned, rebounded off the glass box, and careened at a steep lean toward the guardrail. His motorbike struck the railing and he front-flipped over the top of it. For ten long and torturous metres the Original Australian tumbled, toward a rugged expanse of rocks and shrubs and trees. The somersaulting native hugged his fur-skin bag to his chest, covered his face with his forearm, and slammed onto the ground, prompting a worldwide groan of 'Oooohhhhrrr.'

PART III
THE COAU
XVIII

Crijji woke in a bright and glistening room that looked to be made of sunlight reflecting off water. His head and eyes throbbed. His body and limbs rang with pain. When he tried to speak, the words plopped out like dead frogs.

In time, his awareness came to him. He learned that his arms and legs were swallowed by huge white cocoons, and that there was hard water all around him. He was looking at glass but didn't know it.

Soon he had some visitors. They were White Fricks. Only... they were darker than he'd expected. They were more like Brown Fricks. There were five of them, sitting around him like he was a campfire, and looking at him expectantly. They could speak his language but not from their mouths – their mouths said something else, something foreign. The words that Crijji could understand came from an object much like the one that Albad had. It looked to be made of mica, and was unnatural in shape: It was rectangular.

The remembrance of Albad made Crijji recall the last time he'd seen him. It was in that crazy place where all those people were; when those giant evil flies had chased them. Crijji's first words to the Brown Fricks were, 'Where's Albad?'

'That's the name of your friend, is it?' said the centre-most Brown Frick. He was in his early sixties, thickset, and had white springy hair. He would later introduce himself as Liam Walrik, the Managing Director for the Nation of Original Australia. Liam paused before delivering the news delicately. 'Your friend was taken back to his country. We're all very sad about that.'

Crijji felt sad, too, knowing that Albad wasn't here, and that he was all alone. The feeling reminded him of the many months he'd spent trudging on his own.

'We did *wanna* bring him here,' said Liam, obviously noticing Crijji's reaction. 'But the flamin' COAU government and their heavy-handedness... It's a tough life if you're not white.'

Crijji, at the mention of a word he thought he recognised, asked, 'W-white Fricks?'

The Brown Fricks all chuckled when their own mica objects told them what Crijji had said. Apparently he'd said something cheeky.

'Yes, the White Fricks,' said Liam, amused. 'That's probably not the appropriate thing to go around calling them. (At least not to their faces). White *people* is perhaps a better term. You will in your time see plenty of them.' With curiosity, he asked, 'What is your name?'

'Crijjibah Clibe,' replied Crijji.

Liam nodded as though Crijji's name was a proud fact worthy of note, then introduced the four other Brown Fricks, whom he called The Traditional Representatives for the Nation of Original Australia. 'But just call us TRs,' he added. 'Much easier.'

All of them were in their sixties, except for an athletic-looking man in his late thirties, named Shaquille. Given his youth he was introduced last. Before him came Rosita, who wore a red scarf around her neck... Smacka, who looked like a slightly younger version of Liam, that is, thickest and with springy white hair... and Dave, a bearded man who was paler than the others. They were all friendly, and glad to be meeting Crijji.

'Did you know, Crijjibah. Is that how you say it? Crijjibah? That you're the first person to have left Original Australia and made it to Contemporary Australia?' Liam was so impressed he was almost lost for words. 'The chasm you have crossed is... well, it's a chasm that wouldn't exist, if not for some pretty hard-hearted mentalities that are out there. We've been waiting a long time for someone like you, young Mr Clibe. You're someone who can change the way a lot of people think.

'Is there anything we can get for you? Would you like a drink of water?'

Crijji realised how thirsty he was. His throat felt like it was made of paper bark. He nodded.

Liam showed him how to use a machine sitting next to his bed. Of course Crijji had no idea what either of those things were; all he knew was that the bed was the softest thing he'd ever reclined upon, and that the machine provided the coldest water he'd ever tasted. It came through a flexible plastic straw that bent toward his lips when he asked for it. He remembered what his uncle had said about the White Fricks: how they had magic that could blow up a person's head if you tried to understand it. Already it was obvious that his uncle was right and the elders were wrong. He wondered, as he had many times, if maybe the elders had lied about their knowledge of the White Fricks, and if so, for what reason?

'A lot o' people wanna meet you, Crijjibah,' said Liam, after Crijji had finished drinking. 'The headman of the COAU; even *he* wants to come around and say g'day. D'you think maybe you'd be interested in doing a thing called an interview? That's where ya talk to someone who asks you all kinds of questions. Good questions – nothin curly. Does that sound like it might interest you?'

Crijji gave no reply.

Liam stood and wandered over to the window. Looking out of it, he said, 'There's even people out there holdin' a vigil. Reckon they're not leaving till you're out o' here, which, could be a couple of weeks, the doctors say.' He paused a moment, then said, 'It's good to see all that good will. Was startin' to think it's not out there.'

When the TRs finally said goodbye and departed, Crijji was attended by Magic Men called doctors and nurses. Not all of them were men, though – which was surprising. Most of them were indeed the colour of teeth. And sometimes their eyes were the colour of the sky. Crijji had never seen eyes like those before. They were eerily unnatural. The doctors and nurses must have felt the same way about Crijji, who was black as charcoal and had wild grease-infused hair. The way they looked at him... they seemed to think he wasn't quite real.

There was a lot of food here in the White Frick World. And it came to a person at the same time each and every day. A thin tabletop slid out of the wall next to Crijji's bed, bent around, and delivered a meal in a plastic container. And if Crijji wanted something additional (which he invariably did) all he had to do was say, *Ay, Menu man*, and order it.

On his third day in this place called a *hospital*, he remembered the delicious food that Albad had given him: *Joglud*. Crijji requested some, and when given it, took a bite, and instantly summoned the memory of when he and Albad had decided to cross the border. Albad had joked that Joglud was the reason why Crijji wanted to defy the boundary line. Really it was because of the White Fricks. That those people who now so frequently tended to him had once been mysterious forms, not even proven real... it made him realise how much his world had changed.

Crijji soon learned there was a limit to the amount of Joglud a person could eat. He tried ordering his fifth round for the day but the tabletop said he'd exceeded his quota. He felt a huff of indignation and thumped the tabletop frustratedly. A burst of pain exploded through his casted arm. *Ah, buckin, chit!* he cried out, the agony immense. The residual insult was that he still didn't get any Joglud... until the TRs arrived. They brought him a bag of the stuff, having seen how much he liked it.

Because of Crijji's accent, he called the TRs DRs. These Brown Fricks came almost every day, and usually brought him things that they guessed he might like. They told him that he and they were connected, in that they belonged to the same nation. It was their job to oversee that nation: they were its caretakers; its helpers; its custodians. Crijji was confused that they kept using the word *we*. They seemed to be saying that he and they belonged to the same tribe. He didn't know how the elders would feel about that. They would probably call them devil men for saying such a thing.

As the days continued, the doctors and nurses shone lights in Crijji's eyes, or got him to wiggle his fingers and toes. They were pleased with his progress, and said it should only be a few weeks before he could leave. One of the nurses saw his frustration at being so confined, so showed him how to play video games on his phone. A whole new universe opened up for Crijji. Beamed straight into his eyes were all-consuming terrains filled with obstacles and challenges, villains and allies. In a video game he could do far more than a normal person. He could even fly – just like a magic man. Crijji became so possessed by this White Frick wizardry that he grew irritated whenever someone said he had to break away from it. He even grumbled at having to pause his game when the COAU headman came to visit.

The TRs nervously awaited the headman, their White Frick clothes richer and cleaner than ever. Liam walked back and forth throughout the room, always asking people to repeat themselves because he hadn't properly heard them. Finally the headman arrived. But before he did, glass balls hovered into the room and scattered to various points throughout it. Crijji remembered the media pods from the time when he, Jarl and Migail (as he called them) had been chased by that big allichopter. Now, as before, the pods hung in the air, their appearance like water drops, and blended in with everything else in the room. It was remarkable how quickly Crijji forgot about them.

When the President of the COAU finally arrived – preceded by a group of people, among them some of the head doctors – he was revealed to be a well-dressed man in his late sixties, who smiled easily and shook a lot of hands. He came to Crijji, saw that he couldn't shake hands because of his plaster casts, and instead, held up a fist of solidarity. Liam introduced them to one another. The President welcomed Crijji to Contemporary Australia, and told Crijji he was a highly honoured guest. There was a tinge of sheepishness to the statement: as if the headman had said something he was embarrassed about. Crijji didn't know what to say, so said nothing. That was his standard for the entire visit, unless a mumbled yes or no could relieve the attention pressing in on him.

Crijji wasn't much interested in what the headman had to say. He was keen on getting back to his video game. The President remarked upon the significance of the event, calling it hopeful and historical. Crijji thought about the great white shark he'd been flying through outer space, his feet in stirrups, a machine gun in his hands. He understood nothing of those things – stirrups, sharks, guns, space; he just knew he could have fun with them.

Finally the President said goodbye (holding up another fist of solidarity) and left Crijji to his recovery. The head doctors and other people followed him out, Liam and most of the other TRs going with them. Only Shaquille remained.

'How was that, eh mate?' said Shaquille. 'Pretty good?'

'Yez,' said Crijji, severely uninterested. He'd already returned to his game.

Shaquille wandered over to the window and looked out through it. 'Far out,' he said. 'The crowd's really givin' him a serve.' He produced his phone, filmed for a few moments, then showed the footage to Crijji. Crijji prised himself away from his video game for about two seconds before returning to it.

A short time later, Liam walked back inside and said, 'I think that went well. Whatta you mob reckon?'

The other TRs all agreed.

'And the crowd. Goodness gracious. Jeez did they give that old Prez an earful. Shakkie ya shoulda heard em. One bloke kept sayin' "This is on you, mate. This is on you." He could barely get into his car, poor bloke.'

'Lot o' responsibility, *that* job,' said Shaquille. 'Tryin to keep everyone happy.'

'Yeah, stuff that,' said Liam. 'But, I spose it's what they sign up for.' Turning to Crijji, he said, 'How's our good friend Crijjibah Clibe going?'

Crijji was too preoccupied to answer. Liam waved it away with a smile.

'Dunno how long the flame'll keep burning for,' said Liam. 'Their enthusiasm'll probably die down pretty quickly.'

'Aw I dunno,' said Smacka. 'They seem pretty activated.'

'The activated activists,' said Liam, with a chuckle. 'And not that we can hinge our bets on em. There were plenty back in the day. Public sentiment: bit of a tricky thing to gauge.' Bringing out his phone he looked at the time. 'Alright, I've gotta go. Take it easy eh Crijjibah? I'll swing in again soon.'

The meals continued coming, always ample, and tasty unlike anything from Crijji's world. The doctors and nurses came to see him every day, and talk to him about his broken arms and legs. When they felt he was ready, they set him up with an electric wheelchair. It was shiny like polished ivory, quieter than a hunter, and freed Crijji to zoom throughout corridors, testing the chair's accident avoidance program to a most professional degree.

The day finally came for Crijji to leave the hospital. The TRs loaded him onto his wheelchair, got behind it, and deactivated its drive mode. Liam pushed it out of the hospital room and down the corridor outside. Doctors and nurses lined the walls, applauding as they waved Crijji goodbye.

The glass doors of the hospital's main entrance rippled and peeled apart like curtains drawn away from each other. Outside were thousands of people, so eager to see Crijji that they would have lapped up onto the hospital steps were it not for the line of policemen holding them back. They cheered fervidly when the small plastered figure in a wheelchair was brought before them. On all sides, the colours red, yellow and black thrashed around like agitated schools of fish. Crijji knew what the colours signified. On his first day in the White Frick World Liam had shown him a three-coloured image with a yellow circle at its centre. 'These are the colours of our people, Crijji. The red represents the sand of our deserts, the yellow is a rising sun, and black is the colour of our skin. This is our flag, mate.'

Liam held up an arm and waited for quiet. It came after a powerful up-draught of applause.

'Thank you everybody,' said Liam, his voice amplified by a microphone pinned to his collar. 'Thank you so much for coming here today. To see so many people expressing good will, when for so long it felt as if there was none... it really makes a person dare to hope that... that maybe times have changed.

'Two-and-a-half weeks ago, a young man crash-landed into this nation's consciousness in a way that nobody else ever quite has. His name, he told us, is Crijjibah Clibe; and he comes from a place so buried by time that most people don't even remember it's there. The country this country is built upon is rarely ever thought about by most Contemporary Australians. Until something happens, and they find it *has* to be thought about.

'It's been a long time since anyone dared to hope that an Original Australian might make it to Contemporary Australian soil. For the better part of a century the policies of a former age have excluded them from this nation. Apparently Original people weren't ready for a "modern" country. It was too complex, too overwhelming, too damaging. And maybe such voices were right. For was it not a concrete highway, artificial to the natural land, that this young man tumbled off? Was it not the machinery of modernity that quite literally pushed him? Yes, it was; and yes, he is damaged. But look at him. He's healing. And I believe his example will see other things heal.

'Original Australia is one of three nations that tore into being when a country that was evolving instead fractured. The Great Trifurcation, as it's known, cast from the heart of old Australia its very first citizens. Like blood from a wound they flowed, gathering in a place beyond our view. So many capabilities to be cultivated, so much potential to be harvested... and yet they became a forgotten field. A field that nobody seemed to have any faith in.

'Many in this nation will say Crijjibah Clibe is an omen for disaster; a harbinger of chaos. They will say he should be returned to the country he belongs to. But I ask you to see him differently. I ask you to believe in him: to believe he has the ability to choose for himself what is best for himself. This simple act of good faith will extend to him a dignity denied his fellow countrymen, and strengthen him as he ventures into a strange, strange land, seeing it through eyes most ancient.

'I've told you what others see when they look at Crijjbah Clibe. Now let me tell you what I see. When I look at Crijjibah Clibe I see a shoot of greenery rising up through the sediment of a bygone era. These bandages upon him, I see them spanning the divide between two different worlds. When I look at Crijjibah Clibe, I think: The barren land is beginning to bloom. The wound at the heart of this nation is beginning to heal. And won't it be marvellous when finally that has happened.

'Thank you.'

Liam was about to push Crijji down the steps and through the crowd, but a blast of applause halted the process. Liam repeatedly said *thank you* but couldn't be heard over the sound of it. Crijji sank lower in his wheelchair, afraid of the unbridled enthusiasm. It generated when they both descended the steps, Liam pushing Crijji into a raging ocean of well-wishers.

In spite of the jubilation there was a tinge of solemnity. People reached out from all angles, reverent and consoling, to touch Crijji's casts or place hands upon his wheelchair. They were quickly taken by a buzzing energy that made them sing, sway in unison, and part as Crijji's wheelchair was pushed through their midst. All around him, thrust as though for him to acknowledge them, were the same three colours, emblazoned upon placards, badges, beanies, hats, scarves, flags, banners, T-shirts... Many items also had Crijji's face on them them.

Shaquille was waiting by the car, surrounded by floating media pods, phones aimed at both Crijji and oneself, and policemen encouraging people to tamp down the raucousness. Shaquille clicked a button on his key. From out of the car slid a metal pad that Liam positioned Crijji's wheelchair upon. The pad retracted into the car, the doors closed, and the crowd outside abruptly looked and sounded as though it was underwater. Crijji watched the White Fricks vying for his attention, and wondered how his tribe would react if a person such as a White Frick suddenly landed in its midst. He could see the little kids staring, the women trying not to, and the men remaining silent... He realised: these White Fricks weren't treating him as a stranger. They regarded him as...something else.

Liam opened the front passenger door and seated himself. Shaquille did the same but took the driver's seat. Both times, when the doors opened, the noise of the crowd elevated for a brief and jarring moment.

Shaquille gently steered through the midst of the throng, which closed in around the car as would a herd of ebullient sheep. When breaking beyond it, and the stragglers at its rim, the vehicle graduated to smooth streets that flowed between the hugest things that Crijji had ever seen. They looked like enormous anthills made out of water, and he feared they might lose their intactness and come crashing down to drown the whole world. He'd seen these things called buildings from out of his window at the hospital, but had never been below to look up at them as he was now.

'So whadja reckon?' asked Liam. 'The speech go alright?'

'Yeah, it was spot on,' said Shaquille. 'Very... statesman like. And organic.'

'That's good to hear,' said Liam. 'Gettin' up in front o' people, ya always feel like you're gonna say somethin' stupid.'

'Nah ya handled it well.'

Their road ascended and became a meandering path lined by fauna native to the region. They were passing through the heart of a city but one would never know it. Tall gum trees hung over the roads, their pale bodies like inflated lightning bolts rising out of the ground, their canopies heavy with olive green leaves. Yellow-flowered cassia bushes reminded Crijji of his country – as did granite boulders that punctuated the raised gardens.

In the suburbs beyond the CBD they arrived at a house like all the others on its street. Standing out the front, on a rectangle of lawn half the width of a lap pool, was a Brown Frick in his early twenties. He was introduced as Ricco, and it was his job, said Liam, to look after Crijji. 'If ya need anything,' said Liam, translated by Crijji's phone, 'just ask him and he'll get it for you. Alright, we'll drop all your gear off, then we'll hit up the embassy.'

The ORAU embassy was a modern glass building surrounded by gardens of native plant life. Standing tall and vibrantly out the front of it was the Original Australian flag. Inside, beyond a marble lobby, there was a maze of glass walls, mounted on which were significant images. Liam, with the TRs traipsing behind him, pushed Crijji past dot paintings... photos of crowds holding up fists... charcoal etchings of Original Australians shackled with chains... and a eucalyptus tree branch encased in glass. 'This here's the remnant of a sacred tree,' said Liam, 'destroyed long ago by a bushfire. Of course the White Man who saved this branch of course desecrated the tree in order to do it, but at least we still have a small part of it.'

They came to an airy section of the building that connected to an outdoor area surrounded by landscaped rock hills. Waiting for them were hundreds of people who began clapping the moment they saw Crijji. Liam gave a short speech, welcoming Crijji to home soil, and then everybody watched a group of tanned men wearing red loincloths, who clacked sticks, and danced around bundles of smoking wood.

Afterwards, people were directed to tables loaded up with more food than Crijji had ever seen at one time. Country music was blasting as everyone got in a line and made their way alongside the tables. The honoured guest was at the front of it, using a robotic arm to pile food onto a plate. The arm, called a helper hand, was a feature of his wheelchair.

Several servings and countless samplings later, Crijji, tired and full yet somehow desirous of more dessert, allowed himself to be pushed around the embassy some more. The biggest of all the offices belonged to Liam. 'Whatta ya reckon of the desk?' he asked, pointing to a swollen slab of timber whose varnish he ran his fingers across. 'Californian Redwood. Pretty much can't get it anymore. Protected species. But there's a family over in America that'a been growing it privately for over a hundred years. Nice eh.'

The next office they visited looked out across the landscaped foot hills. Liam parked Crijji behind its desk, then sauntered over to the doorway, folded his arms and leaned against it.

'Whatta ya think of your office, Mr Clibe? It'll do?'

XIX

Crijji's second public appearance took place at a thing called a *yoonibersidy*. It was a grand old building made out of sandstone. Crijji and Liam were ushered into it then up onto a stage, where they received a standing ovation from an auditorium filled with White Fricks. Liam was grateful. Crijji was intimidated.

Their interviewer was a trendy man in his early sixties. He and Liam each assumed a comfortable plush chair on either side of Crijji.

Liam did most all of the talking, which was good for Crijji because, although the applause had been quite exhilarating, it was unnerving to be the focus of so many people's attention. Crijji's replies, when he gave them, were one-word, two-word, and three-word answers, spoken quietly and without eye contact. Liam, on the other hand, expounded at length.

'The Outervention,' said Liam, 'as the whole injustice is colloquially known, is clearly one of the most atrocious chapters in Contemporary Australian history. Because of it, Original Australian people have been rendered the most overlooked, underprivileged, underrepresented and discriminated-against people, literally on this planet. The walls that stand between them and the rest of the world are like the Berlin Wall but on steroids. And if ever there is going to be change; if ever this behemoth wall is to crumble, what needs to happen is what always needed to happen: There needs to be respect given; dignity granted. The people whose lives are being affected need to be asked, How might your life be bettered?'

Liam went on to make a humble announcement that sent a ripple of energy through the audience.

'The Council of Traditional Original Australian Representatives is putting together what we like to call a Roadmap to Reunification. We call this outline the Four Rs Action Plan, and believe it to be the solution to this landmass' longstanding division.

'The first R stands for Recognition. We believe that Crijjibah Clibe needs to be officially recognised as what he's fast becoming known as: Contemporary Australia's First Original Australian Re-Contact.

'The second R stands for Referendum. We believe that, if the question of bringing the Original Australians back to the modern world, was put to the

Contemporary Australian people, the CO-Australians would stand for what they know is right, and refuse to continue ignoring the country this country is built upon.

'The third R stands for Repeal. Our council wants to see the intolerant, judgmental rulings of a bygone era excised from this country's constitution. We want the discriminatory laws that have caged the Originals for so long to be scrapped, so that they too, like everyone else on this landmass, can live with freedom, and dignity.

'The fourth and final R stands for the Action Plan's ultimate objective: Reintegration. We want to see the Original Australian people granted dual citizenship, so that they can maintain their deep and rich connection to their age-old way of life, but at the same time weave themselves into the fabric of the modern world. We know it can be done. In fact we're sure if it. We know because we're watching it happen.'

Liam smiled benignly at Crijji, who hadn't really been listening. Their audience, which had cranked to a higher gear of applause with each succeeding R, rose to its feet and positively cheered.

In cities all across Contemporary Australia, Crijjibah Clibe's wheelchair was trolleyed into cars, onto planes and onto stages; it was brought out and showcased at dinners, luncheons, get-togethers and fundraisers, then carefully loaded into the next vehicle, always to be shuttled to the front of a mob swathed in red, yellow and black, which always seemed to be chanting, *Recognition, Referendum, Repeal. Recognition, Referendum, Repeal.*

'What we're trying to emphasise,' Liam frequently said, 'is that more needs to be done if the wound at the heart of this country is ever going to heal. That's in fact what we're calling this effort: the Heal the Wound campaign.'

The first time Crijji had flown in an aeroplane he'd been ecstatic. Now it was a common experience. He was tired of it, actually; and not just of aeroplanes but of airports and hotel rooms and White Fricks who wanted to look into his eyes or gently touch his casts. They were everywhere, those people, and Liam always indulged them, even when Crijji was trying to play a video game.

Shaquille was usually the one to pick up the TRs from the airport and drop them home. Crijji was the last of his passengers.

All that Crijji wanted was to be alone with no one talking to him. (And joglud; he wanted joglud). He motored inside the house, through its main hallway, ignored Ricco's wave of greeting, and lodged himself inside his room. A moment later there was a knock and Shaquille stepped inside.

'Here's your luggage, mate. Aw, hell, might be a good idea to clean your room eh? Bit messy in here.'

Crijji was using his wheelchair's helper hand to rifle through a plastic bag on the floor. His eyes were fixed on his phone; on his video game. He pointedly ignored Shaquille.

'Did you hear me, mate?'

Again, Crijji ignored him, until Shaquille waved his hand in front of the video game, breaking its magical hold.

'Ay!' said Crijji, in protest.

'Can I ask you something?' said Shaquille.

'Aw whad??!!' said Crijji.

'Where you're from,' said Shaquille, 'if a person doesn't do what they have to do they suffer right away. Here, a person suffers in ten, twenty years, and then for the rest of their life. And their children suffer as well. I've told you about the Aussieological test, yeah? Well, if you don't pass that citizenship exam, they're not gonna let you stay in the country.'

'I don't give chit bout dat zam,' said Crijji. 'Dis *ma* country.'

Shaquille refrained a moment, then said, 'It's not anybody's country, Crijji. We're all just riding this planet. And a thing can only be "owned" until someone with a bigger spear comes along and says otherwise.

'Something you should probably remember, as you listen to all the talk that goes on, is that things don't stand still, even though we want em to. And maybe ask yourself: what's the point of moaning about things that can't be changed?'

XX

Three days before Crijji had left the hospital, Charles and Mihail, who were staying in a different ward, had received a visitor. Liam Walrik had stepped past the two security guards stationed at their door. In his hands was a gift basket. From his mouth came a proposition, related to their appeal of seeking refugee status in the COAU.

'See public attention is a bit of a wild animal that no one can really control,' said Liam, to the broken, bandaged men whose casted limbs were elevated. 'But we can throw a bit o' meat here and there, to see if it might get the scent. I also think it's a bit like a lightbulb. You've got those two points, and they chuck electricity back and forth between each other, and the more they do that, the brighter the light shines. The day you fellas tumbled off that highway with Crijjibah Clibe is the day the lights went on in this country. Y'flicked the switch, and now what we've gotta do is concentrate on passing all that electricity back and forth, so that things stay illuminated. Can ya see what I'm trying to get across?'

'We can indeed, Mr Walrik,' said Mihail. 'And your words remind me of a phrase I think you might appreciate: *Public interest never dies, it just gets buried alive.*

'We were hoping someone like you would pick up a shovel and join us. If we had the use of our arms and legs, we'd propose a toast.'

XXI

Shaquille and Crijji were at the airport, waiting to catch a plane. Crijji was playing a video game in which he was he was driving a military tank through the streets of a chaotic city. He broke from it when suddenly realising:

'I'm ungry.'

'Y'can't be hungry. Ya just had a massive feed not long ago.'

'Nah I'm ungry. I wan joglud.'

'I think y'been eating enough o' that rubbish, Crijjibah. Too much isn't good for you.'

'Noao, I wan more. I'm ungry!'

'Maybe on the plane, eh? We'll be on it pretty soon. Make your order now, from your phone.'

'Na das too long! I'm ungry now!'

The plaster-casted Original sat in frustration for several moments, then flung about restively and motored away. Shaquille sighed, got to his feet, grabbed hold of both their suitcases, and followed him.

The wheelchair-bound native zoomed through the midst of fellow travellers, some of whom recognised him and pointed him out. Shaquille, managing to not lose sight of him, followed him all the way to a food court.

Crijji parked himself at the front of a line and leered at the colourful glazed delicacies on the other side of a glass visor. The many gridded levels of donuts, cakes, eclairs and muffins was a tantalising display. Crijji activated his helper hand and tapped excitedly on the glass. A man buying a latte saw his desire; and a few moments later the Original was clutching a delicious donut with pink icing and colourful sprinkles.

Shaquille, arriving upon the scene's conclusion, grudgingly said, 'Whatta ya say to the gentleman, Crijji?'

Crijji looked up at the well-wisher with the latte, and said, 'Milgjake?'

Several days later, Crijji went to a local wildlife park, where, as well as getting some sunshine and fresh air, he could see some familiar animals. His two minders led the way into a nocturnal exhibition. Inside it were reptiles and marsupials in glass terrariums. 'Ab look,' said Crijji, tapping on the glass with his helper hand, and chuckling. 'Dey god little oppices.'

At lunchtime, Ricco used an embassy card to buy Crijji a hamburger, a large carton of French fries, a drink called a choco-cherry blast, onion rings, a muffin, and a cup of blue jelly with crackling sugar dust inside it. His other minder, Kaylana, who was a petite young woman with squiggly dark hair, gawped at Crijji's meal and said, 'Surely he's not gonna eat all that.'

'You wait,' said Ricco.

With the aid of his helper hand, Crijji ate his monstrous meal and chugged down his drink, then burped half internally and said, 'I wan ice cream.'

'I don't think that's a good idea, Crijji,' said Kaylana. 'You've had quite a bit. We should see more of the park first.'

'Nah. I wan ice cream!'

'Maybe we should just get him one,' said Ricco. 'He's gonna go off his brain otherwise.'

'Well, let him,' said Kaylana. 'Do you know how bad all that stuff he's eating is? Especially for blackfellas. Their kidneys practically explode when coming into contact with modern food.'

'Did you just call him a... *blackfella*?' asked Ricco.

'We're *allowed* to, Ricco,' Kaylana tartly said, as if it was obvious.

'Ay!' said Crijji, sparing Ricco from having to give a reply. 'I wan ice cream!'

When Ricco shrugged as though he was powerless to intervene against the will of Kaylana, Crijji growled, grabbed a paper cup with his helper hand, and slang it away from their table. The cup sailed through the air and landed on the ground near another table of people. Crijji was pleased with the distance he'd achieved, but not with pursed-lip expression on Kaylana, which silently insisted that such activity would not get him what he wanted. Crijji would fix that. He reached out his robotic hand, collected all the empty cartons and wrappers, squeezed them into a tight wad, then flung it. There was a swelling pause in which nobody complied... And then Crijji yelled, grabbed the entire lunch tray, and ditched it!

Later that afternoon, at the ORAU embassy, Crijji, in his office, was whirring around recklessly, avoiding any collisions thanks to the on-board mechanism in his wheelchair. There were many obstacles to steer around, such as guitars, didgeridoos, and a drum kit (all given to him to bring out his musical potential). There were the scattered keys to various cities, and sundry products sent by respectful and admiring corporations. Crijji laughed as he motored through all of these hazards, touching none of them as he whizzed around and around and around.

In the office across the hallway, Liam, seated behind his redwood desk, was about to begin talking to a holographic news anchor. To their vast audience the two men were seated in the same room, at televised a "Table of Conversation."

'You've probably seen the footage,' said Dennis, emphatically moving his head from side to side, 'or you might have just heard about it. Either way, Original Australian Ice Cream Outrage has become an internet sensation. Posted only three hours ago, it has had over 400 million views. With me today is Liam Walrik, the Managing Director for the Council of Traditional Original Australian Representatives. Liam, thank you very much for joining us.'

'Thank you, er, Dennis. Thanks for having me.'

'Now, the position your council is taking, is that Crijjibah Clibe's behaviour today was a result of... sugar.'

'That is correct, Dennis. We believe that Crijjibah Clibe has been using food – particularly sweet food – in an effort to self-medicate. There are many issues he's dealing with at the moment, not just in relation to his injuries. You see, as he's learning about this new country he's crash-landed into, he's learning about its history, and is having to come to terms with it. There is a great backlog of pain, grief, trauma and injustice that he's all of a sudden become privy to. It's a heavy load he now carries. And today's incident is a reminder of its true weight.'

'Of course this type of adverse reaction to the modern world,' said Dennis, 'is precisely what a lot of people have been worried about. Was the writing not *on the wall*, so to speak?'

'I think the people who take that approach,' said Liam, 'adopt a superficial perspective, and fail to see the real reality, the one beneath the surface. I also believe it's the duty of people such as myself – a proud Original Australian – to try and help them see differently: to try and help them question if... if maybe there's more going on here.'

'So today's occurrence,' said Dennis, 'it isn't raising any alarm bells for you?'

'I think "alarm bells" is a very strong phrase, Dennis. Has today's occurrence made us re-evaluate our approach in regard to dealing with Crijjibah Clibe? *Yes*. Has it made us more mindful of the delicateness of this unique situation? *Yes*. Has it convinced us to increase our efforts; to see that the right thing is done by this young man? *Absolutely*. But what it's mainly done, is revealed to us the degree to which Crijjibah Clibe needs acceptance and support, given how greatly he's been affected by the country built upon *his* country. And that's not just a job for our council, Dennis. That's a job for all of Contemporary Australia.'

'Do you think Crijjibah Clibe understands,' said Dennis, 'what it means to have a healthy lifestyle? Has he been warned about things like diet, and congenital ailments?'

'We've told him that too much of certain things – of anything – is bad for a person.'

'So there *is* now an onus upon him, then.'

'I wouldn't word it in such a way as that, Dennis. I'd say, *There is still much more that Crijjibah Clibe has to learn, and it's our job to provide him with the support and education he needs and deserves as he undertakes the challenge of entering a new and foreign world*. But let me just make a point of saying: something that we at the council have learned, both from this experience and from other experiences, is that, people need to understand: *Yes* Crijjibah Clibe needs to go easy on the sugar – but that's *his* decision. We at the council can't be expected to force feed him nutritious food – that's simply not our place. We can encourage, and advise, and guide – but we can't impose our values on him. And yes today's incident is something worthy of note; but it isn't something to be discouraged by. We're *excited* about Crijjibah Clibe's future, more so than ever; because while he's encountered setbacks, he's also made a lot of progress.'

'We're going to take a look at the infamous footage of Crijjibah Clibe,' said Dennis, 'which was posted online early this afternoon. I must warn viewers, it is quite confronting.'

High definition footage beamed out of Liam's phone, showing an irate Crijjibah Clibe racing around in his wheelchair, his helper hand swinging wildly as he picked up rubbish and threw it at tourists. His profanities were constantly bleeped out, however a few racial slurs made it past the censors.

'Liam Walrik, Crijjibah Clibe doesn't appear to be very happy, does he.'

'No he's not happy, Dennis. And a person has to ask *why* he's not happy. (And it's got little to do with ice cream). Right now, Crijjibah Clibe is dealing not just with physical injuries, but with spiritual injuries. He is learning that, in the same way that he is shrouded by bandages, and trapped by plaster casts, his people are shrouded by unjust policies, and trapped by a divisive rule of law that has plunged them into an unqualified dark age. Crijjibah Clibe stands between two worlds; he occupies the very Wound in need of Healing. But the wound *of* that Wound is inside him. And for one to Heal the other must heal. If Contemporary Australians truly do want to Heal the Wound at the Heart of this Nation, Dennis, they need to do it with more than just sentiments. As it stands, the document calling for an end to Australia's division has been signed by only a handful of CO-Australians.'

'You are of course referring,' said Dennis, 'to the petition seeking to have Crijjibah Clibe recognised as the COAU's first Original Australian Re-contact.'

'As you know, Dennis, when Europeans first made contact with the Original Australians, it took a long time for them to even recognise Originals *as* Australians. We believe the people of Contemporary Australia will have more insight than their forebears; and we also believe a speedy acceptance of Crijjibah Clibe will mean the same for *all* Original Australians. That of course would signal a whole new era in the CO-Australian psyche. Whether CO-Australians are prepared for that, well, that's a different matter.'

'And after the recognition of Crijjibah Clibe,' said Dennis, 'would come the referendum seeking to repeal the Outervention laws. You would have it that Original Australia and Contemporary Australia are rejoined.'

'Our ultimate aim,' said Liam, 'is to see the Original Australians afforded the same opportunities as everyone else on this landmass. But that can't happen if they are excluded from the rest of the world. At the moment, our petition for Crijjibah Clibe's recognition has about 300 thousand digital signatures. That's a substantial amount, but, not nearly enough to make a real difference. On that basis, I would beseech the CO Australian people, to ask themselves what kind of nation they hope to belong to. One that ensures a just and equal future for all people? Or one that continues to abide in a profound degree of intolerance?'

'And just to let everybody at home know,' said Dennis. 'The details for that signature list can be found at www.orau.com.coau. I take it Crijjibah Clibe's name is on that list?'

'Well, he can't yet hold a pen, Dennis. But I'm sure that when he's able to, Crijjibah Clibe's name will be at the top of that list.'

'Liam Walrik, thank you very much for appearing on the programme.'

'Thank you, Dennis. I appreciate the opportunity to make things clear and understandable for the general public.'

When the holographic news caster disappeared, Liam rose to his feet and headed for the door. The office across the hall was his destination. Arriving at it, he knocked, and slipped inside despite hearing no answer.

Crijji was immersed in a video game, held before his eyes by his wheelchair's helper hand. The faraway look on the Original's face made Liam wonder if interrupting him might cause some kind of neurological fit.

'Hey Crijji? Mind if I talk to you for a second?

'Would you mind pausing your game?

'I just need to tell you, mate, that if you start feeling frustrated, you've gotta let people know. Okay? When you start feeling agitated, you've gotta tell people. Alright?'

'Would you mind pausing the game for a moment?

'Crijjibah?

'Crijji?'

'Whad?'

'Did you hear what I said?

'I asked if you'd pause your video game.

'Did you hear me?

'Crijji?

'Did you hear what I said?

'I'm just gonna...'

Liam reached out and gently plucked the phone from out of the helper hand's fingertips. The reaction was instantaneous.

'AY! I'm gon lose d game!'

'I just need to talk to you for a second, Crijji.'

The helper hand clawed at the air, seeking to snatch back the phone. Liam sprang backwards, aghast and affronted, clutching the phone to his chest. Crijji motored toward him for another attempt, the robotic arm retracting in order to spring forward. Liam scurried behind the desk, putting it between them, and circled around it whenever Crijji tried to make a move for him. The several partial rotations, one way then another, so infuriated the Original that he balled the fingers of his helper hand into a fist and shook it acrimoniously.

Because the glass walls of Crijji's office were not switched to an opaque setting, the situation quickly had an audience. The council employees senior enough to intervene stepped inside, these being Smacka, Dave and Rosita. It wasn't till Shaquille arrived that someone had the foresight to opt for discretion. He flicked a switch near the doorway and the glass walls became foggy, much to the disappointment of the dozen or so people gathered outside in the corridor.

Crijji was screaming unintelligible sentences, punctuated by the words *gimme ma buckin bideogame,* and was picking up anything he could find so as to throw it at Liam.

'Whatta ya reckon?' said Shaquille. 'Is there a protocol for this sort o' thing?'

'Probably not the time for jokes, Shakkie,' said Liam. 'Here, Smacka, catch this.'

Liam threw the phone to Smacka, who threw it to Dave, who threw it to Rosita, each passing it along when Crijji spun his wheelchair and rocketed toward them. When Rosita flung the phone to Shaquille, he simply put it in his pocket.

Crijji turned and raced toward him like a swaddled demon in a sprint car, his helper hand pulled all the way back. He slang the hand with all of his mental might; it leapt as if launching a shot put. But then, it froze in mid air, and the wheelchair suddenly braked. Crijji would have spilled out of his seat had he not been belted in. Realising that his wheelchair wouldn't function as he intended, he lunged for the phone with both of his casted arms. Again, he was prevented by the restraints of his wheelchair.

The rage inside Crijji crashed against the plaster he was constrained by. His body shook and wriggled as he clenched a scream between his teeth. The wheelchair came back on line, he reversed a fraction then accelerated forward. Once again the wheelchair deactivated.

Liam watched the anguish Crijji was enduring. The young man was motoring back and forth, spinning in circles and braking violently. It was hard to watch. His cries of frustration were hard to hear. Liam couldn't endure much more of this.

'Aw look Shakkie just give him the bloody phone, would you?'

'Are you serious?'

'Course I'm bloody serious. Just give it to him, would you? We don't wanna be causing this amount of upset. He's been through enough.'

Crijji had stopped motoring around. He was sobbing, whimpering, and muttering, *buckin DRs*.

Shaquille said, 'I don't think we'll be setting ourselves up for a win if we hand it over now.'

'Na it'll be alright,' said Liam. 'Just give it to him.'

'I really do advise against it.'

'Shakkie, just give it to him, would you?'

Shaquille provided an underarm throw that returned the phone to Liam, saying, 'I might let you do the honours.'

Liam caught it then hurried over to Crijji, knelt down next to him and said, 'Here y'are, Crijji. Here y'go, mate. Look, it's your phone. Y'want it?'

At first Crijji wouldn't accept the phone; his demeanour said it was far too late. But finally Liam managed to place the device in the helper hand without it dropping. The robotic limb pinched hold of the phone, swivelled round, and positioned it at a good viewing angle. Within moments Crijji was once again absorbed in a video game.

The TRs stood back and conferred, their tone like mourners at a wake.

'I think he's overtired.'

'Yeah it's been a big few weeks.'

'Probably needs a bit o' downtime.'

'Home time's probably a good idea,' said Shaquille. 'I can take him if you need.'

When the other TRs all filed out of the office, Shaquille made his way over to Crijji's unused desk and sat down on it.

'Hey Crijji, just give us a yell when you wanna go home, eh?'

There was no answer... not until half an hour later, when Crijji, having woken from his video game, knocked on the glass door of Shaquille's office and said, 'Ay. I'm ungry. Les go.'

For a long time they travelled in silence, Shaquille calmly steering, Crijji looking out at the native shrubs lining their road. Shaquille finally asked, 'Hey Crijji, do you know what a musical is?'

'No,' was the answer, after a long pause.

'It's a thing where people tell a story using songs. There's one I think you might like. Can I send it to you?'

'Ib you wan to,' said Crijji, answering in a language not his own without even realising it. This he did quite often, because the White Frick language was gradually becoming comprehensible to him.

They arrived at Crijji's house and found that Ricco had made dinner. Crijji ate it with enthusiasm, then committed himself to wheelies and burn outs, which he performed both inside and outside the house. Before Shaquille left, he sent Crijji a copy of the musical he'd mentioned, and encouraged him to watch it, saying he'd enjoy it.

Several hours later, when Crijji grew tired of playing video games, he navigated to the musical and began watching it, motivated more by boredom than curiosity. It was called *Anthropia*, and it told the story of a man living in a time called the Divided Age. Crijji soon realised it was more about the age than it was about the man, and that Shaquille had sent it to him for a very simple reason: its relevance.

XXII

It came to be that when Crijji rolled down city streets, backed by crowds festooned in the colours red, yellow and black, he imagined his supporters holding him up on their shoulders, wheelchair and all, to carry him with reverence. He was an object charged with sacred worth, to be followed wherever his casted, unblemished hand might point. That these followers were committed to the cause of the Original Australians was something Crijji had come to doubt. He saw them as committed to the worship of their own totem.

Crijji had learned that the Original Australians were widely regarded as *totemites*: people who believe they have a mystical connection with a spirit-being such as an animal or plant, and who use that item as an emblem or symbol to bind and represent them. The term was usually applied to primitive peoples, but since watching *Anthropia* multiple times, Crijji had learned there were no bigger totemites than the ultra-modern White Fricks.

The White Fricks' totem was a golden tree reaching for a kingdom in the sky, its leaves shining brightly like beacons, its soil available nowhere else in the world. There were many fruits to be found upon this tree. Crijji, it seemed, was one of them. When the White Fricks rallied behind him, it was as if they were holding him up as proof: proof of what *could* bloom, proof of what *had* bloomed, proof of what they *allowed* to bloom. Crijji, like many other kinds of people, was evidence of Human Flourishing.

At first the White Frick totem had been buried beneath arguments. Nobody saw the shape of it, or its growth, because they were too busy looking at the conflicts it caused. Shrouding it were gauges going haywire, their pointers spinning back and forth from one definition to another. It wasn't till Crijji's third viewing that he took the time to learn about the properties being measured. His understanding in some ways improved, but in other ways became muddled. He soon realised that all a person really had to know about the Divided Age, was that beneath the barbed bickering there was a phantom monument being raised. It had a long and deep shadow, and a gravity that pulled people into a customary spin. The White Fricks' newest maypole was a lightning rod for their energies. To it flowed their tributes, in the very same way that the initiates of Crijji's tribe offered up their blood.

The White Fricks' totem had ultimately fallen – at least in its most vibrant state. Thanks to its very upholders, it had twisted, snapped, and crashed to the ground, spilling its many fruits. But apparently its seeds had taken root. As Crijji was trolleyed to wherever he was required to be, he looked around and always saw counterparts to the characters in *Anthropia*. Evidently the song and dance of the devotees had resumed – without people even knowing it.

It was curious, the way that the ideas of *Anthropia* now overlaid the world as Crijji saw it. It was as if a pair of spectacles had been placed in front of his eyes, and through them he could see a metaphorical reality. He'd learned about the word *metaphor* by way of a lyric describing the totem as *the metaphor dictating the semaphore.* On learning about *semaphore,* he realised he could see a form of it all around him. Faces, words and actions transmitted a clear message: *We have our chosen object. It's time for a ceremony.*

Crijji trusted gatherings less and less, owing to how madness could simmer in a mob, and how stampedes could be steered by riders clutching reins. He feared that, if the Whinge of Change had already begun blowing, *point, paint and pounce* might soon become the protocol. He could easily imagine marchers and spectators opposing each other like performers in a dance-off. One group would pantomime the tamping and hurling of explosive words; the other would react as if mortally wounded. Both would stomp toward each other, jaws jutting and heads wobbling, impending screams brimming. Their clapping collision would bring a swirling throng of dancers whose movements would become ever more vicious. In a sped-up moment there would be nothing but chaos.

Crijji was so besieged by thoughts that his mind no longer had room for trivial things like video games. Most of his time he now spent thinking, or learning. He'd lock himself inside his room or office, and partake of documentaries about whatever subject he felt was relevant. The information was unending, and delivered in his own language – unless his language had no relatable words, in which case he had to learn the White Frick words for the things being described. In doing this, he began to generate a picture of where the White Fricks had come from, and grew ever more certain that their heritage, and in fact the heritage of all peoples, was key to understanding their present-day compulsions.

Recognition, Referendum, Repeal; Recognition, Referendum, Repeal...

'If anything is ever going to change, what needs to happen is...'

Crijji felt the TRs were ushering people toward the Maze of Absolutes, the walls of which were either black or white and never a gradation, not until suddenly they became completely grey, as if neither black nor white existed. Shaquille wasn't much help in this hour of confusion. He told Crijji that anything he did from here was his own choice, and supposed that, like the White Fricks of old, Crijji's battle was between Restraint and abandon; between Firm Ground and Faith. He was referring to the Reintegration of the Originals, the calls for which were becoming louder and unrelenting.

Alone in his office, trying to grapple with all he was learning, and trying to gain a bearing on which direction to take, Crijji abruptly realised that his understanding of the past – about the reasons why three different countries had formed – had been framed by the TRs and those who agreed with them. There must be more to the story. When listening to news articles, it was obvious that, in the present age, any discussion relating to Crijjibah Clibe had the potential to light up into a squabble. How could so many people disagree so sharply if the picture they all looked at was perfectly clear?

Crijji resolved to learn unflinchingly about the reasons for the exile of the Original Australians. The Outervention was a subject he currently knew very little about. He would change that – even if it proper traumatised him.

XXIII

Liam and Shaquille were sitting in the former's office, analysing details related to the council's most recent acquisition. The plot of land had long ago been an Original Australian sacred site. Presently it was a car park; but that was going to change. The TRs intended to restore it to its original function.

'Hang on Shakkie I've just gotta take this call. These blokes'a been after me for a while now and I've been too busy to talk to em. Don't worry it won't take long.

'Hello there, Mr Mihail, how are you going, sir?

'That's good; good to hear. And they're treating you well, there at the– facility?

'Good. Good. Yeah me, I'm fine. Flat out like nuthin else, though – with this whole Recognition mandate. Gonna be worth it, though. Hey look sorry for not tappin' heads till now; I woulda got in contact sooner but, as I said, we're busy as all-anything over this way. What can I do for youz? Need a referral, heh heh.

'...

'No, no I haven't checked that out. What is it again? I'll make a note of it. *World of peace.com.coau*. Yeah right; yeah I'll have a listen. Be good to hear the whole story.

'Aw ya did, eh? That's nice to hear. Yeah Crijji speaks fondly o' you blokes, too.

'Publicly? Yeah I'm pretty sure he has. He's *always* talkin' about you fellas. I am, too.

'...

'That *is* strange. Maybe you just haven't been on the right sites, or been on the right channels.

'...

'Yeah I can imagine they *have* loaded you up with a bit o' free time. Even still, though; ya shoulda come across *me* sayin' a few things. I feel like I'm *always* bangin' on about you blokes. Though backstage is probably where I do most o' the heavy lifting, 'cause audiences, they're pretty sensitive these days. They arc up if they feel an agenda gettin' plugged.

'I will, though; yeah. Yeah I will; I'll be a bit more overt. Nah don't worry, ya haven't faded into the background. Nah not at all.

'Hey look, I've gotta run, 'cause I'm hard pressed with all the priorities, but whatta ya reckon one day I bring Crijji in and we have ourselves a photo session. We could even have a sit-down interview sort o' thing, like we did just recently with the... gawd I forget the name of it; there'a been so many. I imagine it's the same with you fellas.

'Yell out if ya need anything, yeah? Anything at all – even if it's, I dunno, socks, haha. Original Australia owes you two blokes a great deal o' gratitude. Y'brought back one of our own.

'Alright then. Take care then, eh? I'll be in touch. Yeht, righto, righto, yeht; you too. Alright then I'll catcha later. Soon. Yeah. Will do. Yeht. Sounds good. Alright. Alright good. Catcha later then. Yeah for sure. Bye. Bye.'

Liam ended the call and said, 'Hoo. That was an earful. Pretty good English, that young– whatever-he-is.

'Alright. Where were we?'

XIV

When are you gonna sign the petition? Liam would ask, Smacka would ask, Dave, Rosita and all the council employees and volunteers would ask. Crijji would always demur from answering; and Liam, if they were in the presence of unfamiliar people, would jovially change the subject. An idea had been put forward: to have the signature list printed out on paperbark. 'Not the whole list, obviously,' said Liam. 'If we did that it'd be the size of a car.' Several versions were submitted for the approval of the council. Crijji was included in the process but expressed no view.

Hanging on the glass walls of the council offices were photographs of pre-Outervention TRs. Crijji had mostly ignored them. But now he looked at them closely. He questioned the people's motives, and also their effect, what with all of their controversies, and how every indicator of Original wellbeing had plummeted under their leadership. Crijji had concluded it was probably smartest not to trust them. His reasoning was simple. These men and women were the kind who would talk at length about the Stolen Generation, yet fail to once mention the Rescued Generation.

The documentaries about the Outervention had changed Crijji. Profoundly. He could never again view his country as he had; he could never again see his people as he had. Bewildering graphs and statistics had made him feel dizzy. Descriptions of horrible occurrences had made him feel sad. He didn't know how to process all of the besieging information, so, to try and untangle his thoughts, he used *Anthropia* as a template: he imagined the Outervention as a musical.

The stage was in the shape of the Australian landmass. Filled with black performers dancing calmly, it lurched and rocked when a wooden ship filled with white performers barged into it. The black performers staggered and stumbled as the ground beneath them heaved. Their dance became unruly and out of control. Eventually they all fell and lay on the floor, where they wrestled, or struck themselves relentlessly, or lay totally still. Around them sprouted industrial factories, their chimneys pumping banknotes, soon flaming banknotes that ever multiplied. The factories grew fatter and fatter and finally popped. From out of their rubble rose the bony markers of the ORAU, meaning the white performers could no longer dance among the black performers. All this time the stage had been reeling, but now it stopped. The black dancers got to their feet, looked around as though awakened, and resumed their calm dance.

The Original Australians had been removed from modernity because they were maiming themselves with it. And now people like the TRs wanted to restore them to that modernity. Crijji doubted the wisdom of such an ambition, what with all the chaos the documentaries had shown him. Truly it was a nightmare. There were images he wished he hadn't seen, and stories he wished he hadn't heard. The Originals of the Divided Age had lived in torment.

There was something else Crijji had learned that had shaken him profoundly. It related as much to the present as it did to the past. The animals that had saved Crijji from death; the animals he thought had been sent by magic men... they were robots, deployed from out of the ground when imminent violence was detected.

Crijji's skin grew mottled when he remembered the King Brown snakes slithering across the dirt, and how their raised heads had opened to reveal horrible mouths and nasty little teeth. Even now, insulated against the natural world by walls and floors and ceilings, he was terrified by those snakes, and how they'd hissingly told him to *Run*. But to think they weren't even real; that they were machines engineered by the White Fricks... it made him feel as if all the world had suddenly been revealed as something false. Of course not all snakes were artificial – just the ones that intervened on his behalf. Like the rest of the animals of that night, they were sophisticated balloons with spindly metal skeletons that dictated their movement. They remained deflated till the moment they were needed, then flew to the site of the conflict, to use exaggerated body movement and loud noises to coerce their subjects toward calm. That the animals were mainly made of air seemed to worsen the insult. It made Crijji's fear of them seem ridiculous.

Crijji decided to stop ignoring his wheelchair when it recommended exercises and for light degrees of pressure to be exerted upon his broken limbs. He allowed the chair to unfold into an upright pose and gently set his casted feet upon the floor. From there he walked around like a woozy reinforced toddler, making sure the glass walls of his office were opaque so nobody could peer inside and watch him. He also refrained from eating so much bad food.

This he did because of something he'd imagined: a huge pile of lollies standing tall before his desk, melting into a liquid puddle that he dipped his face into and drank from. Standing in a queue behind him were all the Originals who might drink as he had. There weren't just a few of them. There were generations of them; and if they drank of Crijji's poisonous waterhole, they'd be consumed by a raging dance that would only ever stop when they were violently torn away from it.

In spite of all the changes inside Crijji, the world around him continued as it had. Healing the Wound and Bringing the Originals Home comprised the exalted vision. A current of beaming faces carried him from one part of the COAU to another; from one protest to another; from one private meeting to another. The hope and expectation on all sides of him formed a pressure almost tangible. Crijji didn't want to disappoint all these people who so believed in him and the cause he represented, but he increasingly felt he was going to have to. He'd decided that he couldn't put his name on the petition to bring back the Originals, not when it was helping to unleash a mayhem presently arrested.

But then, something unexpected happened, and people acted as if it was the most marvellous thing in the world; as if history had taken place before their eyes. Liam was the one who broke the news to Crijji. He knocked on the door of Crijji's office, slipped inside and said, 'I have something pretty fantastic to tell you, Crijji. I've just gotten off the phone with the President of the COAU. He's decided to recognise you as the First Original Australian Re-contact: the first of your people to make your way back.'

Liam seemed to expect Crijji to leap out of his wheelchair and shout with exultation. Crijji of course didn't. He said nothing, and considered what all this meant.

It meant the White Fricks had chosen a tribal point of focus and were directing their energy toward it. It meant a rolling wave had perhaps got started, one that could pick up Crijji's people, and dump them catastrophically.

Liam was talking but Crijji wasn't listening. All that Crijji could think about was that he, as the First Re-Contact, was perhaps little more than a key for unlocking carnage.

XXV

Crijji didn't want to be recognised as anything. All he wanted was to go back home to his people and live among them for the rest of his life. But he couldn't do that. They'd kill him the moment they saw him, protective animals or no protective animals. He'd broken the law, and his unfulfilled punishment was by no means nullified.

But if his people could see the White Fricks were real... would they forgive him? He'd questioned this many times, and had frequently imagined bringing to his tribe a White Frick representative, someone they could look at closely. If they accepted the person, or maybe even people, surely they'd abandon their desire for a reckoning. Crijji wanted to believe this, but *Anthropia* had taught him that people can be blind to things right in front of them, all because the tiny electric rivers in their minds flowed to places they'd already determined them to.

The casts were taken off his arms and legs, the wheelchair was returned to the hospital. Upright, and at eye level with most others, he relished his ability to move freely again, and questioned what he would do with this freedom. The White Frick world held less and less interest for him, probably because, now that he wasn't gorging himself on chocolate and distracting himself with video games, the full weight of his isolation was apparent. He missed his people deeply – so deeply that sometimes he wished he wouldn't wake up. He could hear their voices and see them laughing. He could imagine the way they'd react to all the crazy things here in the White Frick world. Crijji would love to introduce them to this world; but haunting that prospect were the nightmarish symptoms which had so impacted the Originals in the past. To see that plague carry forward into the future...it would be heart-breaking.

Crijji had told Liam that he wasn't going to sign the petition. Liam had said, 'Crijji, what about your people? They're cut off from the world. Don't you wanna see them being all they can be?"

'Maybe das ow it should be,' said Crijji. 'Dey should be cut opp prom ebryone.'

'Maybe just keep having a think about it, eh?' said Liam. 'What you're talking about is a big decision, with a lot o' consequences.'

Crijji said he would, and neither had mentioned the subject since that time, not until Liam said, 'Hey if you're not gonna sign the petition, would you mind handing it over? We were gonna do that at the Recognition ceremony. That's not too far off now. Only a couple o' weeks. You *are* gonna come to that, yeah?'

Crijji said he didn't know; that he hadn't decided. Liam nodded and said nothing more.

The council's conference rooms were always opened up and occupied with volunteers and visitors. Badges, flyers and stickers were pinned and plastered abundantly. The glass walls played an eternal loop of celebrity endorsements, sometimes interrupted by updates about the vigil at the ORAU border.

The place where Crijji and Albad had cut the citizen chips from their hands had become something of a shrine, one that would only decamp if the COAU government agreed to hold a referendum. Burning candles stood atop the white markers, graffiti blemished them broadside. There were drums, didgeridoos, dancing and body paint. Someone had sculpted and raised a statue of Crijji, looking into the distance and holding up a bleeding hand. That soulful image was often tattooed onto people's skin.

The dedication of the festival-goers was greatly esteemed by the TRs, who often visited the site and thanked everybody for all their hard work. This same esteem carried Crijji; and he knew that if it was to vanish from under him, the experience would be comparable to when his tribe had suddenly turned against him. He didn't want to endure that again. The disappointment in people's eyes would be too much for him.

XXVI

And so, on the evening of the Recognition ceremony, Crijji allowed himself to be dressed in a three-piece suit whose lapels were three familiar colours, and to be gathered up in a limousine and taken to one of the tallest buildings in the city. There, at the top of it, in a vast ballroom that seemed to have no walls; which was nothing but a polished wooden floor that appeared to be hovering, he looked out across a lumpy field of incandescent seeds, and a mountain range that looked like a granite tidal wave sweeping through the city. In the westward sky the sun was melting on the horizon. In not long it would be dark.

Men in tuxedoes and women in shiny fluorescent dresses made their way throughout the function room, between tables that moved as if they were floating upon oceanic currents. Taking their places behind gleaming silverware, they sat beneath a glittering canopy of stars that became punctured by shafts of pale light. These beams illuminated dancers in red loincloths, who ran throughout the ballroom telling an ancient story. Crijji watched them from the other side of a veil made of tiny, interlocking, almost invisible glass beads. It concealed him from the people beyond, and would open up when it was time for him to be introduced.

On the other side of the room, a pale column of light shone down from the stars, illuminating Liam, who ascended a stage that had risen from the floor. People applauded and then Liam began speaking. As he did, he moved in Crijji's direction, the light following him, the stage beneath him moving to catch his feet. Tears shone in Liam's eyes. His voice choked with emotion. He was talking about the people the nation had forgotten and the future inheritance of coming generations. Crijji heard remodelled repeats of things said on prior occasions, and remembered words from *Anthropia*:

> *Here now comes a noble priest*
> *To teach one how to offer*
> *To satisfy a god on earth*
> *And bring the kingdom proper*

The paperbark petition in Crijji's hand suddenly became so heavy that he wanted to let go of it. He wondered if the resulting *thunk* would awaken anyone. Probably not. Looking out at the pale faces surrounding him, he saw people who were transfixed, and knew that the gravity of what possessed them was so strong that light would bend and sound would distort. They would be blind to what they didn't want to see, and deaf to what they didn't want to hear. They were willing captives of their idol.

Crijji understood that the present ceremony was not to celebrate his "return", but to laud the form on which he grew; the form that stood behind him. Crijji was a fruit of the golden tree; and if he wasn't standing here to represent it, somebody else would be. The characteristics of that somebody were reducible to three ingredients: they needed to be Vulnerable, they needed to be Individuated, and they needed to be an Other. They needed to demonstrate one's power to offer protection; the capacity of humankind to evolve into a distinctive form; and they needed to be different, so that by the embrace of them a communion would take place. This communion would catalyse the rising of human kind. It would lift the branches of the idol so it pierced the soil of a land where all could gather in peace. A collective vision of harmony, and a transfiguration that would achieve it, rumbled in the minds of the White Fricks. They pined for this paradise, and prompted each other toward it. Their song and dance revolved around it.

Liam said Crijji's name and suddenly a spotlight was shining down on him. The White Fricks stood to their feet and applauded, their hands creating thunder, their eyes glistening in the low light. The concealing veil had disintegrated, letting through a wave of admiration so strong that Crijji wavered where he stood. The petition he clutched... soon the President would come for it. Crijji suddenly regretted that he would be the one to hand it over.

The reason was simple. Crijji feared that the current song and dance was nothing but a primitive loop, and that the White Fricks were regressing into a circular canyon carved by the footfalls of their ancestors. In the past they had paraded around their Vulnerable Individuated Others, protecting them zealously, and using them as evidence of their own ethical soil. Ethical soil was the reason for the ritual. Their VIOtem pole, as it was known, could stand nowhere else in the world, and was a proxy for the golden tree. As the White Fricks poured out libations at its base, they wanted for the flame they were building to rise and unfurl into glorious branches. Instead they shone a light onto a new and strange religion. At the top of the VIOtem pole was an image singularly Human. Neither this nor that but everything simultaneously, it represented both the Freedom to bloom into a glorious desired state, and the ultimate object of the White Fricks' devotion: their species.

By this point Liam was standing alongside Crijji, beaming at him with affection and pride. The President got up from his seat, made his way over, climbed the same stage and joined them. First he shook Liam's hand, then he shook Crijji's hand. When the President released his grip, Crijji meekly held up the petition, feeling light but at the same time heavy as the President took it from him. Liam nodded firmly and thoughtfully, as if telling Crijji he'd done the right thing. Crijji felt ill. He remembered how the many faces of the VIOtem pole had opened wide, their maws demanding more; and how the pyres built around them were loaded up with offerings but none was satisfactory. An insatiable megalith of dissatisfaction had been created. The eye of the totemnado had been seeded.

As the updraft of applause continued, Crijji wondered how much of it was genuine and how much was coerced. An ocean of rolling eyes might well be latent in the people gathered round him. The only things holding it back might be the fear of a primate reaction, and the desire to not hackle the wood grain pointing inward. The media pods hovering throughout the room reminded him of Trial by Swarm and the Cosmopolitan Inquisitions: times when hot lights had greeted language infractions and examples were made of dissidents. It was imperative that the tribal object only be illuminated by glowing hearts held high for all to see. Anyone who failed to do so dragged the world into darkness. They were the discordant, and discordance would not be tolerated by the Harmonists.

The applause finally quieted. The White Fricks took their seats. As Crijji listened to the President's speech, hearing words that had been sown all over the country, he mused at how seeds had floated out of mouths then taken root in minds, there to repeat the process and fill the world with their kinds. That process – the replication of oneself – was central to the proceedings. The White Fricks were Makers of Rain, Bringers of Harvest. The crop they sought to conjure was more of their own kin.

A pretty young woman ascended the stage, in her hands a varnished wooden case, inside it a gold medallion. Presently, Crijji was awarded the title of *Contemporary Australia's First Original Australian Re-Contact*, and there hung from his neck a testament to this status. Fervent applause rose and finally diminished. Crijji, feeling numb, said the only words required of him: 'Dang you berry muj.'

The President returned the stage to Liam. Crijji heard nothing that was said. Around him was a wispy whirlpool of pale dancing ghosts. To signal a New Age, and draw a cleansing line between Now and Then, they shook their heads at their forebears and held their arms out wide, exhibiting both The Want To Be Embraced and The Distance We Have Come. These people of the past were raising the symbol of their faith. Together they chanted,

Join us and be led
Trust us and be raised
Believe in us as we believe in you
May the Oneness now be praised

Oneness was inviolate: the ideal that could not be questioned. Any who disputed it, or suggested cracks in its form, were the sinners of the age: the darkened and the ignorant. Crijji looked out at the encircling crowd and could see the optic of Oneness glinting in people's eyes. The world's newest graven image was a fountain of holy flesh, its generations rising to the heavens in a surging upward rally. This great and beautiful bouquet was filled with people of all kinds and colours. Crijjibah Clibe was a testament to this, and evidence that all could be absorbed. *Absorption or dissolution; make known your allegiance!* That demand simmered beneath the ceremony, ready to erupt in yet more displays of devotion. Crijji could almost feel its power vibrating through the floor. He half expected for cracks to appear, just as they had all around the golden tree.

Apparently nothing more was required of Crijji. Liam gestured for him to dismount the stage and make his way to their table. He did, and as he sat down another performance began. Colourful beams and splotches of light exploded all around. Crijji barely noticed. Looking at the space where he'd been standing, he pictured himself surrounded by the Radius of Respect – a sweeping protective line that allowed him to stand as one set apart. This sacred circle he occupied was a buffer against chaos, employed because the future could not look like the past. In the past, tribal warfare had engulfed nearly all the world; and this could happen again, far worse because of the powers since acquired. The recognition of Crijji was a safeguard. As an anointed representative of a people group, Crijji not only pronounced the differences between groups, but erased them, by making the groups part of the same exhibit. The White Fricks were demonstrating that all are different, yet all are the same.

Liam returned to the stage, no doubt to supervise another ceremonial recalling of wrongs. Like others of his lineage he'd scented the power of the object – the power channeled by the tribe – and had stepped into the Radius of Respect to serve as a connected intermediate. Crijji's leg started bouncing up and down. He remembered people lashing themselves with planks pulled from one's own eye, and their exultation when olive branches were set on fire and waved around to fill the world with smoke. He imagined Liam with a glinting medallion similar to his own. It was in the form of a wide open mouth. Liam clutched it with reverence as the Whinges of Change blustered all around him, and scowled with umbrage that anyone might dare question his sanctity. Before Liam were placed offerings of expiation. He turned his face away from them, allowed them to decompose, and then took the rotting hunks of un-forgiveness and kneaded them into the tribal mind. The White Fricks danced around Liam and his VIOtem pole, calling out *Bow!*, calling out *Behold!,* and splashing the pigment of darkness onto those who would not fold. But the joke was on Liam, and indeed on Crijji, who had allowed himself to be placed upon the object of ritual. When the White Fricks danced around the VIOtem pole, they were dancing around the golden tree. And when they danced around the golden tree, they were dancing around themselves. For in the White Fricks' fable they were the trunk of the mighty idol, dutifully carrying all others skyward.

Sometimes Crijji almost hated the White Fricks, for how they could use a person as a lynchpin in their Welcome to Anthropia ceremonies. And it wasn't just people they used. In faith that Anthropia would settle upon the world, the White Fricks had looked across the face of the Earth and confessed on it all their sins, that in the tending of them they could stand on ground made holy: ground *they* would make holy. Their idol rose from a tabernacle blue and green: from the third element in a trinity of temple, idol and heaven. This gargantuan scapegoat would receive their darkness, and, when they had cleansed it, complete the righteous circuit. The Mother, Dream and Holy Post would all flow into one another, their unity a Natural system.

Crijji clenched his fingers, strangling them with one another. He could see in his mind how the White Fricks' dance could become orgiastic, how their intensity of focus could create a blazing axis point. As before, the Total Item would want to shine brighter than any other form, and would bend then cast back any light that might degrade it. The object at the heart of the tribe would become the mind of the tribe. Even more, it would become the stomach of the tribe. To it would be thrown offerings, to be seen and to be heard. The congregation's conflagration would rise, its misty scions rich in hue. The beauty of the outcome would make the sacrifice worth it.

Crijji needed to get out of here. There were too many eyes wanting to connect with his for a shared human moment; too many people wanting to display their Tears of Empathy, those glimmering jewels adorning the modern-day halo. While it was still dark enough that he would remain mostly unnoticed, he rose off his chair and moved away from his table, bent over to avoid attention. That was impossible, however. On all sides of him were table-loads of White Fricks, basking in the warmth of a reflected self. They suddenly applauded at something. Crijji flinched as though struck. He was sensitive now to the raising of a regnant reality: distrustful of it. Muck had been labelled firmest ground in flowery orations, and blood had watered the tree during Enlightenment demonstrations – even though the object was twisting against its roots, swelling with the Yeast of the Pharisees, and leaning unhealthily toward sugary constellations.

Crijji felt as if the room was going to explode: as if the clean slate laid by the White Fricks was again about to rupture. He could hear the crinkling of the tin foil sheath as lungfuls of hot air inflated the totem. He could see thorny tangled arguments clambering all over it, while against it crashed waves standing or sitting in their ovations. But nobody here seemed to remember all this. To them the tree was bright and shining and upright, not a writhing, groping Medusa, puncturing the only womb in which it could ever grow.

Searching for an avenue of escape, Crijji found it at the edge of the room, where a rectangular blur throbbed against the city skyline. He hurried toward what he knew was an elevator, hoping that no one would intercept him. He could imagine a tide of pale faces rushing over to see if he was alright. With it would be Liam, thanking people for their concern before directing their attention toward the choir about to begin sobbing. The doors opened and Crijji stepped inside, thankful and relieved when they closed. In calming silence he pressed a random button, and waited for the doors to open. When they did, he was surprised at what he saw.

XXVII

Stars were heavy in the sky, and all around were pale thin gum trees. At first Crijji thought this flat parkland was some kind of illusion – as with the walls and ceiling of the ballroom lower down. But fresh air breezed gently across his skin and trickled through the olive green canopies. This place was genuinely in the open.

A network of hovering glass bulbs cast pale wedges of light onto blocks of stone lined up neatly. A surge of fear clawed at Crijji when he realised what the stones were. They were markers of where dead people lay buried. This place was what the White Fricks call a cemetery. But what was a cemetery doing on top of a tall building?

The answer quickly built itself, courtesy of what he'd learned about the Divided Age. All around the city were suspended slices of a bygone way of life, cut out of the ground and elevated many decades ago because of rising land prices and compromises about the preservation of heritage sites. The Originals weren't the only ones who'd found themselves in a changed world. Many White Fricks had been just as disorientated.

Crijji was grateful when something not too far away caught his attention. It looked like a black-and-white campfire hovering in the air. Intrigued, he made his way toward it, over stones that crunched beneath his shoes. He soon understood that he'd glimpsed a hologram playing ages old film footage. Only then did he remember the main reason for why the Recognition ceremony had taken place at the function room beneath. Interred at this cemetery was Australia's First Aboriginal Citizen.

Albert Namatjira's grave was marked by a staunch monolithic sandstone a little bit taller than Crijji. On the front of it was a tile reproduction of one of the many landscape paintings the artist had been famous for. Crijji looked closely at the image, remembering what he'd learned about its creator. Albert Namatjira had been imprisoned in his later life for supplying alcohol to his family members. The New System told him the act was illegal, while the Old System told him that possessions belong not to an individual but to the tribe. Namatjira, caught between two worlds, had made a decision, and a young woman had died on account of drunken violence. His own death was more mysterious. Some believed he'd died at the hand of sinister retributive magic. Others believed he'd died of a broken heart, aware of what the future held for his people.

A heavy question settled upon Crijji's shoulders, asking if one day he too would be the subject of unhappy speculation. He felt the answer was certain. Thanks to the events of this evening, the destination of the path ahead seemed inevitable. His people would be used in further rituals overlaid onto arenas of all kinds... they would bloat and stagger and fumble with the elements of a changed world... they would party as fresh generations walked on broken feet. How could Crijji have taken the first step toward all that? How could he have been so cowardly? He already knew the answer. The power of the tribe.

Turning away from the gravestone of Albert Namatjira, Crijji wandered through the rooftop cemetery, breathing deeply the cool night air, and pondering how one day there might well be acronyms for Before Crijjibah Clibe and After Crijjibah Clibe. If the timeline of the Original Australians was a living thing, Crijji was probably cleaving it with a sword. He grimaced when thinking of how the White Fricks had done the very same thing to the Originals' timeline – and then tried to stitch it back together and proclaim it good and healthy. They were just like the singing doctors with the over-sized needles, whose ligatures held together *Frankenculturalism*. That morbid tribute to the idol had ultimately torn at the seams and collapsed, its fractures defining the Divided Age, and creating the three nations of the Australian landmass.

Crijji came to a balcony looking out over the city, and there glimpsed a familiar feature. The rocky gorge in the city's mountain range, known as the gap, was a natural gateway to the north and south, and had, coursing through it, a sandy riverbed filled with thick leafy gumtrees. The riverbed and the roads surrounding it were currently filled with tens of thousands of people, all celebrating, Crijji remembered, the historic day when the landmass' inland had first been irrigated with controlled vapour paths. Pale rolling clouds filled the gap, crackling and fulminating as though imbued with glitter and colourful radiation. As Crijji listened to the cheering, he remembered why the Recognition had been scheduled for this particular date. The TRs had wanted to remind people that not everyone on the landmass could partake of its prosperity.

As Crijji stared at the gap, he thought of the White Fricks' timeline, and of how it too had been divided, by a lightning bolt who was the unacknowledged armature of the golden tree. He pictured a giant version of the man in his victory/vulnerability pose, standing inside the pyrotechnic mist and keeping at bay the two swells of rock delimiting the gap. The Template, or the Ultimate Advocate, as he was known, formed a bridge with his outreaching arms. Those arms were once a considered passage for the Originals to move from one world to another. But then had come the Humanists, bottling the man's light and claiming it as their own, their performances trying to out-perform. They twisted Judge Not into Think Not, renamed the Gentile, and sought to build a new Body of believers. But their dance had had them reaching for a kingdom no longer with a king; and as their feet shredded old fabric they drilled unwittingly toward darkness they couldn't remove. Had they traced the vertebra of their beloved they'd have been more cautious. Instead they cast their eyes onward and upward, and tapped a wellspring that flooded their lands.

Crijji looked up at the stars, feeling like a man whose map was eroding. As always, words from *Anthropia* whispered to him, speaking of how creatures from the slime had viewed the great surrounding vacuum as a tribute to their climb, and had warmed their frosty hands around the notion of their own spirit. He wondered what kind of campfire he himself could lean toward... and couldn't think of an answer. Drawing a weary breath, he clutched his new medallion. It was heavy, and shiny, and engraved with images he was too distracted to focus on. He suddenly had the urge to take it off and throw it as hard as he could. To some people it signified the power to give, to others the power to demand. To Crijji it signified a gargantuan responsibility.

Still looking up at the night sky, Crijji happened to see the sweeping crescent of white dots that his uncle had pointed out so many years before. He instantly remembered the deep shame and the exile effected by the faraway pattern, and what the elders had said about it being a flock of birds that had flown too high and gotten trapped because of their desire to know everything. That very desire had freed Crijji, at least in regard to understanding a great many things. He'd learned the pattern was actually a group of satellites, positioned above the world to inspire humanity to greater heights. It was intended to be a fully-formed circle, symbolic of unity; however earthly conflicts had stymied that ambition. Crijji mused at how not even that long ago he'd thought the pattern had been made by magic of the highest order. Now it was just yet another contraption – one more component in the White Fricks' prayer mat of gadgetry.

A nearby lightbulb quietly captured Crijji's attention. About three metres off the ground, it drifted like flotsam on a lake, its light creating shadows that swept around gravestones. He had the urge to walk over and pluck it out of the air, slip it into his pocket and take it back to his people. He could imagine how they might react if he brought it out and threw it up to let it float. They would scream in terror and look at him as though he was a demon. And maybe they'd be right. For some reason he remembered that eerie scene where the White Fricks had lined up to lay the insignias of their many tribes onto an altar. Perhaps he'd thought of it because he feared he was just like them. They'd destroyed something in the hope of creating something else. If Crijji was to tear apart the membrane hiding his people from a greater world, he too could bring about mayhem.

Crijji had begun to feel like that character in *Anthropia* who'd treaded between two spinning worlds, destined to be steamrolled if he didn't forgo one and climb the other. Back and forth the man had hopped, or been dragged by the people still onboard, finally to scramble up the face of one planet and let the other float away, its members all disappointed with him. Descending further into his thoughts, he pictured a giant Albert Namatjira standing within the gap, trying with all of his strength to stop two geological bodies from colliding. Crijji understood: if he was to return to his home country, and tell his people about the tribes beyond their own, he would have to pass through the very same gateway that had crushed his predecessor. On one side would be his tribe, on the other the New World, both pushing and pulling at him, and each trying to scrape handfuls of the other so as to feed on them.

Crijji awoke to the world beyond his mind, and fixed his eyes upon the gap. First he perceived it as a giant rip in the mountain range, and then as a huge gouge, made by a monstrous wrecking ball. It made him think that if a new planet was again hurtling toward an old story, the impact would be tremendous. Empty space would meet people's feet when they tried to follow the path laid down by their ancestors. They would plummet. Unless...

In Crijji's imagination, there rolled across the top of the mountain range a circle made of people holding hands. Instead of spinning off into the gap, it broke at a single point, and unrolled into a stitch that spanned the gap entirely. Crijji knew that a shared grip would have to be broken in order to reach for something new. Certain partnerships would have to be relinquished. To bring this about, he saw himself treading through darkness, toward a meagre flame that his people were huddled around. They saw him coming and were angry, not just because of what he'd done, but because of what he'd brought. He deeply knew the only way they would listen to him would be... would be if they feared what he brought.

If the gnarled ancient hands of the tribal elders held up objects made of sticks and rocks and bones, then Crijji, to achieve the respect of his people, would have to hold up something more powerful. Fortunately, that had been provided by the White Fricks.

XXVIII

Sayeed Mihail and Charles Gaco were surprised when the midday news announced that Crijjibah Clibe had unexpectedly returned to his native country. Aerial footage showed the First Re-contact stepping past the white markers of the ORAU border, from there becoming a lonely figure wading deeper into a watery horizon. Charles and Mihail attentively watched the broadcast and all of its attendant discussions, raising plastic glasses several times throughout the afternoon to toast their historical friend. They were accommodated in a comfortable three bedroom house, from which they weren't allowed to leave unless granted permission by their case manager. Clipped around their ankles were transponders – string-wide and tracking their every move.

Several weeks later they encountered another surprise, when Mihail's phone blared the sound of a didgeridoo, and its screen announced that *Liam Walrik* was calling.

'Heh,' said Mihail. 'I wonder what he wants.'

'He might want for to say hello, buddy. It *has* been a long time.'

'I shall indulge him then, Charles,' said Mihail, pressing the *accept call* button. 'Mr Walrik, how are you, sir?'

'That's good to hear. And yes we're well, thank you. Of course both Charles and I have heard about our mutual friend. That must be very hard for you; I know how closely you worked together.

'Yes, well, it's a legacy to be proud of. And I hope you *are* proud of it.

'Well, if you're not proud of it, I'm proud of it for you.' Mihail turned to Charles and gave him a cheeky thumbs-up. Charles returned the gesture with a wide, good-natured grin.

'Oh yes, yes I have heard about that event,' continued Mihail. 'It's quite significant on the calendar of your people, isn't it.

'No, I've never been to one. And I don't think Charles has, either.

'Well, I've never put much thought into it, but, now that I am thinking about it, I'd have to say, it would be something of an honour.

'Oh. Well. I'm... flattered. That would be... an extraordinary opportunity. And again, an honour. Of course I'd have to run it by my Partner in Doing

Time, but I'm sure he'd be delighted. It would be the high point of our stay in your beloved country.

'Well alright, then, I'll discuss it with Charles and then get back to you. Sounds good. Like a plan, yes. Alright. Alright I'll speak to you soon. Enjoy your day. Ha, how can we not? Alright, alright we'll speak soon. Thank you. Ta ta, yes. Goodbye.'

Mihail ended the call, and nodded contemplatively.

'What did he want, buddy?'

'He has invited us to be the guest speakers at his organisation's annual Invasion Day commemoration.'

'Oh,' said Charles. 'That would be very... interesting. Do you think we should go to it, buddy?'

'I think we would be crazy *not* to capitalise on this opportunity, Charles.'

'But he has not been replying to us, no? Why all-of-sudden yes?'

'I wonder about that,' said Mihail, thoughtfully. 'And my suspicions are, he's head-hunting lower down the rungs of the VIOtem pole.'

'Ohhh,' said Charles, who, during the time of their detainment, had been introduced to the musical *Anthropia*, and thus understood the reference. 'We are, how you say, mascots, and, magnets.'

'Precisely, Charles. And rather crude ones, if you think about it.'

'What then do you think we should do, buddy? Should we *be* mascots and magnets?'

'Let me have a think about it, Charles. My intuition tells me, that if we *were* to do a speech, and word it correctly, our website would fatten like a spoiled, stroppy child.'

XXIX

Low-rise commercial buildings and a quasi-developed shopping complex crowded around a normally-vacant lot filled with thousands of people braving the afternoon sun. Those who weren't meandering past information stalls, traditional demonstrations, or a three-coloured marquee in which passports were stamped, focused their attention on a floating slab of a stage. Bounding across it, in front of looped footage showing protesters clashing with police, was a pale man with a shaved head, who was rapping, *'I'm proud o' bein black, I'm never goin back, even though ya tie me down and keep me in the rat track, My race, ya know, my colour yeah it shows...'*

Charles and Mihail were escorted through the crowd by their four-man security detail, assigned not only to prevent their escape, but to protect them against extremists unhappy about their presence in the COAU.

'Don't worry fellas,' Liam said upon greeting them. 'You're in our country now.'

When the rapper finished his performance, Liam clambered onto the floating stage and thanked him, then thanked the attendees for making the effort to be here on this important day.

'Invasion Day,' said Liam, as the crowd grew still and silent, 'is a day of remembrance. We remember the day that the First Fleet landed upon the shores of this landmass, and we remember how a country was built upon another country. Remembrance is important. Not only does it bring focus to the past, but it helps bring focus to the present, and even more, the future. By understanding where we come from, we can understand where we are, and anticipate where we are heading. Because of understanding, we can adjust our course for a land we *want*; for a land that *should* be.

'For tens of thousands of years the land you are standing on was treated with a reverence incomprehensible to the modern person. Original Australians cared for this country, and were connected to it, for generation after generation after generation. But then came the Great Disconnection, and to the lives of a proud and peaceful people came pain, grief, disease, obliteration, decimation, powerlessness and trauma. Were they not warriors, they likely would no longer be. But they *are* still here, ladies and gentlemen. Not only do their descendants continue to walk the earth, but their spirits remain, here in this land.'

All throughout the vacant lot, plumes of mist shot up into the air and spread out to create an impenetrable covering. Instantly it filled out with high-definition landscape images: rocky foot hills that pebbled away to forever, grasslands of tawny spinifex, and corkwood trees so textured they looked as if their bark could be broken off. Most important were the people: dark-skinned men, women and children dressed only in ragged animal-skins. Liam's audience stood in the midst of a tribe so real that tears came to many people's eyes.

'Imagine what life must have been like all those years ago,' said Liam, as people tried to touch the holographic natives. 'Imagine feeling so connected to the land that it's part of you. And then imagine someone coming along and pulling the earth out from under you. Imagine them building these monstrosities we see around us now.'

Certain portions of the artificial landscape disappeared, revealing the buildings beyond the vacant lot, and making it feel as though two time periods had abruptly merged.

'These buildings,' said Liam, 'they only stand because something else gave way. They only exist because something else ceased to exist. And that makes me wonder... To bring about a world we *want*; to make stand a world that *should* be... What might have to give way? What might have to cease to exist? Perhaps it's little more than a calibration of the way we see the world. Perhaps it's something as simple as the map that defines our navigation. If a new bearing is required, maybe it's just a particular mast that needs to be lowered.

'There are many people who can't be here today. And it's them I think of when setting sight on the horizon. Do you know what I see when I take out my spyglass and put it to my eye? I see the flesh-and-blood descendants of these ghosts you see around you now, coming to this small island to commemorate this important occasion. Fervently I hope this is what other people see. Because if it is, there's a chance, a real chance, that in the future, on this significant day, children who right now are isolated from the rest of the world, will stand as fully-grown adults, and here on this sacred ground say to your grandchildren what I say to you now: *Ladies and gentlemen, boys and girls, people from all over the landmass and all across the world, Welcome... to Original Australia.*'

Had people been sitting they would have stood to their feet, such was the enthusiasm behind the crowd's applause. Liam thanked the people, and thanked them again; and then, when they were quiet enough that he could be heard, he asked them to please welcome to the stage the two men whose noble deeds had lit a spark of hope in the hearts of millions across the world.

'Ladies and gentlemen, Charles Gaco and Sayeed Mihail, friends of Original Australia!'

Charles and Mihail bounced up onto the floating stage, both wearing jeans and chequered shirts: Mihail's was red, Charles' blue. They waved enthusiastically at the crowd, which rallied in response. Grinning widely they bowed in many directions; and to Liam they bent a knee and crossed themselves.

'Whoo,' said Mihail, his voice amplified by a clip-on microphone. 'How about that reception, Charles? One would almost think these good people have forgiven us for raising their taxes. All of those added security measures at their border certainly can't be cheap. What *beneficence*!

'In the likely event you've never heard of us, my name is Sayeed Mihail, and the big black gentleman to my left is Charles Gaco.'

'Like taco,' said Charles, his voice also amplified. 'But with a G.'

'And need it even be stated,' said Mihail, 'that we are honoured to be standing here on this auspicious day. More than just honoured, we are invigorated. That audio-visual demonstration of the roaming natives was marvellous – an experience we shall never forget.'

'I have to say, though, buddy. I am surprised we did not see any megafauna. What do you think happened to those big furry animals?'

'I believe the natives ate them, Charles, which is surprising, given the whole PR plopping of *harmony*. Of course there *is* debate about the causes for the megafauna's extinction, but, when *isn't* there debate? Case in point: those peaceful indigenes driving out the pesky pygmies who happened to be living on the landmass first.'

'Oh not the Little People,' said Charles, '(of whom I have seen photographs). Is Little People the right word for them, buddy?'

'I think it depends on who you ask, Charles. Me, I'm fine with the term. But then *term* is such a *harsh* word – it reminds me of prison. And *that* reminds me of the horrible daytime television we've been forced to endure in our eminently comfortable lodgings, provided of course by you fine people.'

'The CO-Australians have been *very* generous to us, buddy. I wish there was, how you say, some way we could *give back* to them.'

'Hmm. Perhaps there is, Charles. Perhaps we can give them a... a sense of proportion. And perhaps we can do it in a manner in keeping with the day's nautical theme.

'Because I'm not chummy with anyone in the audio-visual department, I'll ask you all to please *imagine* the tribe we encountered not too long ago, and see it "culturally unmolested unto the present day." Culture, I have been informed, can be distilled to the following description: *The Way We Think We Do Things*. An example might be: *Leave behind to die, in the wilderness, any superfluous infants.*'

'Hmm,' said Charles. 'I don't remember anyone ever commemorating the *Superfluous* Generations. Perhaps we can get some funding to start a movement.'

'Right after we look toward the horizon, Charles, and imagine rolling across it A Big Chubby Threat To One's Ancient Way Of Doing Things. And it can't be the Great White War Machine so powerful that it took two-hundred years for its drivers to even realise it was an army they'd run over. No no, the last thing we want is to fan the flames of false humility. Retrospective nasal-gazing is little more than a veiled form of ancestor worship. Because the only thing worse than being talked about, is *not* being talked about. Paint me in pathos and call me pathetic, that's just my opinion. But anyway, Charles, imagine for how long sticks and rocks and time-honoured traditions would last against someone in say a tank. The way I see it, 1788 is a year to be grateful for.'

'Buddy, I am outraged, and I *do not* want you to explain yourself!'

'What you call Invasion Day,' said Mihail, 'I call Inevitable Day – which is a far milder phrase than others I've heard, such as, Aborigines Took a Few Bullets But Dodged an Atom Bomb Day. How long would it be, I wonder, before a landmass rich in minerals like this one simply became too much of a temptation for The Powers That Be Elsewhere?'

'Not long, buddy. But all of that is hypothetical, remember.'

'Until of course we put it to the test, Charles, and see what happens when the surveillance cameras are turned away for an extended period of time. Why, what some groups would do with the décor, would make it feel as if *1588* was the year to be commiserated. May we all be grateful those witch-hunting stake-burning torture-artists never made it to these abundant lands. If they had, our indigenous friends might never have learned to complain. And speaking of complaints. The fact that in this country they don't come fifing out of open windpipes is music to my ears. Isn't it lovely, Charles, that no one in this crowd is holding up a sign saying *Behead those who insult Captain Cook*.'

'It is very nice for us to see, buddy.'

'So nice,' said Mihail, 'that I almost feel welcome enough to say, *Contemporary Australians, on this day we exhort you: Lower your fences and open your gates, that people like us can s-wamp your society!*'

Both men simultaneously ripped open their chequered shirts then tore them off with a flourish of the arms. Underneath Mihail wore a T-shirt imprinted with a bandolier of dynamite, while Charles wore what seemed to be an apron, one that rolled off his midsection to reveal a necklace of shrunken skulls and a grass skirt.

'You'll be happy to know,' said Mihail, 'our traditional garb was purchased with CO-Australian money. Those who would like to complain can sign onto our website, *www.zkplight.com.umcau*. While you're there, perhaps also sign our petition asking for the borders of the UMCAU to be expanded *just this one more time*.'

'We promise this will be the *last* time,' said Charles, disingenuously.

'I suppose we'd better wrap things up, Charles. We don't want miss the latest episode of *What Might Have Been*. Yes I know you say it's a painfully hypothetical program, but I do maintain: the juxtaposition of a circumstance with a *potential* circumstance can actually be *very* educational. Liberating, even. I mean think about it. Comparison can be the thief of joy, but it can also bear the fruits of gratitude.'

'Have you got any examples for us to nibble on, buddy?'

'They're all around us, Charles. One can see them every time a news update blares its horrible wares. But perhaps I only see them because I'm a transplantationalist – able to plant oneself in the shoes of another. There are many who don't seem to have that ability. Allllllllll of their focus goes to the proverbial Number One. Meanwhile:

'People are starving, wars are raging, there are more slaves in the world than ever before, pernicious ideologies sweep the planet, and freedom is more-often yearned-for rather than treated as natural and squandered. In a world in which greed and cruelty naturally reign, there are countless individuals clamouring to find safe havens. And there are other individuals around whom safe havens have risen. To the latter group – which could be in danger of thinking itself exempt from the whole equation – I think I might advise: perhaps pick up that spyglass and have a look around at some of the other countries on this planet. I'm sure that if you do, you'll arrive at the very same conclusion that Charles and I have come to: You'll feel very fortunate, very lucky, very blessed and very thankful... that we were not on those boats when the First Fleet landed. Thank you.'

XXX

Shaquille knocked lightly on the door of Liam's office and entered when there was a grunt from the other side.

'How y'goin'?' he asked, sitting down in one of the chairs facing Liam's desk.

'Aw look, y'know,' said Liam, his face heavy, his eyes tired. 'Still recovering from those flamin' UMC ratbags. Can you believe they've started their own showcast? All the people who wanted 'em out, now tune in like nothin' else, and hold 'em up as flamin' model citizens. They're even tryin'a *help* em get citizenship. Just goes to show eh.'

'Well,' said Shaquille, 'they do say that values are the building blocks of tribes. Nothing new there. I have had a listen, though, to their show. Whatta they call it?'

'The *Refuse-to-agree Refugees*,' said Liam, shaking his head.

Shaquille also shook his head, although with a faint smile. Liam saw it and said, 'It's not funny, Shakkie. The damage those blokes have done is... big.'

'Y'sound tired, uncle Liam.'

'I am tired, mate. I've been fighting for the OR-Australians for...'

'For all the time you've been alive.'

Liam nodded pensively.

'Y'think that's healthy?' asked Shaquille.

'I think it's necessary.'

Shaquille refrained a moment, then said, 'Really?'

'You don't?'

'I dunno,' said Shaquille. 'The only thing I *do* know is, people gettin' all riled up, it's not good for your body; puts your heart under pressure. Stress is poison. I look at all those outraged demonstrators and think: *you buggers are all poisoning yourselves.*'

'Well, *I'm* still here,' said Liam.

'Lookin' about ready to drop dead,' said Shaquille, with quiet cheekiness.

'Well, if I do... Aw I'm too tired to think of anything funny to say.'

They both laughed.

'Where to from here?' Liam finally said. 'That's *my* big question. Carry on like nothin' happened, or, keep on answering all the impertinent queries from journos etc?'

'Well, as they say,' said Shaquille, 'respect in moderation is good, 'cause then y'don't get hooked on it.'

'I shoulda cut the microphone on those mongrels,' said Liam. 'And flamin' Crijjibah Clibe, goin' back to his home country. I *can* understand it: missing his family and everything. But after all the work we did, to just, turn away from it...' He exhaled wearily and sat in silence for a time.

Shaquille sat with him, but finally said, 'Y'*can* always go and visit him. Do a doco. *In the Wild with Liam Walrik.*'

Liam laughed in spite of himself, saying, '*Live from Original Australia.* We cross now to our foreign correspondent, Youngfulla Shakkie, who's just caught himself a goanna.'

'Yeah stuff that,' said Shaquille. 'I'm not comin' with ya. I'd perish on the bitumen, let alone out in the scrub. Give me refrigeration and running water any day o' the week.'

'You're a coconut, mate,' said Liam, jibing him good-naturedly.

Shaquille was quiet for a time, then said, 'I used to get confused by all that, when I was a kid, 'cause people are *red* on the inside, not black or white. And then I realised: it was all about the colour of somebody's mind.

'You remember what that fella once said about the Original flag; that when he sees it he sees black, white, and a brown circle dividing 'em?

'He also reckoned that when people went looking for the First Australians, they shoulda set their eyes on the old Half Castes, 'cause they symbolise the merging of two totally different worlds.

'Y'ever wonder if the Wound that really needs Healing, resides in that big brown circle?'

Liam's eyes narrowed. He took a slow breath and replied, 'I think it's a complicated issue, Shakkie. And I have got a *lot* of work to be doing. But anyway what's with the philosophising?'

'Aw I've just been thinking about a lot of things. Y'know, which fights to pick, which ones to flick.'

'You'll never go wrong fightin' for your people, mate.'

'Unless they're gettin' flogged 'cause they gotta pull their heads in,' replied Shaquille.

Liam gave a wince of a smile.

'You're right, though,' said Shaquille. 'It is all complicated. And I don't pretend to know anything about anything. But at the same time, I remember this illustration I saw once, of a helicopter, or it was like a gyro contraption, but anyway, it had blades made of fingers pointed outward, and when it took off into the air the fingers made it spin all wrongly, and finally of course it fell apart and crashed. I've always found that a really helpful little picture.

'Anyway, boss,' said Shaquille, standing and making for the door. 'Spose I better leave you to it. Have a good weekend, eh? Don't work too hard.'

Liam frowned as if the conversation had been a curious one. Shaquille gave him a thumbs-up, then closed the door and left him on his own.

Part IV
Return to the ORAU
XXXI

Crijji felt as though every pore in his body could suddenly breathe again – as if nutrients he'd been deprived of were soaking through his skin. This must have been how Bennelong had felt when he'd returned to Australia from England. He'd been the first of the Originals to ever travel with the White Fricks, on a big wooden ship that sailed across the ocean. What a different world that had been to the one that existed now. It was the same in one distinct way, however – a way that always impressed itself upon Crijji's thoughts: it was a world merely floating on the soil, and could very easily sink.

The land was so powerful that Crijji was amazed by it. It was unfamiliar country to him, so he didn't know any of its stories, but the way it rose and fell and spread out to forever, its colours rich and fiery against the never-ending sky... It made him feel like that Jesus bloke who'd walked on water, only this water was stormy and frozen in time, a geological roar made visible.

The greatest danger Crijji faced was probably from other tribes, whose people would be suspicious of any foreigner. But he had with him his phone, which allowed him to trace any Originals he might be proximate to. He could run if anyone got too close to him, and plot his way through different countries. He sometimes held back a wry smile when remembering what a White Frick politician had once said about a United Original Australia: It was an idea beyond rich, given how sometimes not even beloved football matches can withstand the conflicts between family groups.

The microchip that Crijji had cut out of his hand – which had an equal buried beneath the skin of *every* ORAU citizen – was on display in a White Frick museum, alongside a signed photograph of the scruffy man who'd found it. This meant Crijji couldn't rely on it in times of distress. If a snake bit him, there would be no antidote delivered by a robotic wasp. If he failed to catch any animals, he would go hungry. It was a daunting prospect, mainly because sometimes animals were scarce... but he'd firmly resolved that if a wedge-tailed eagle carrying game flew too close, he'd grab that medallion from the White Fricks and ditch it at the bird.

Crijji sometimes wondered if the future would have him selecting people to help form the equivalent of a university. It wouldn't be like that one in the cartoon, though – an abandoned derelict husk labelled a *University for the Un-interested*. No way. This one would probably be beneath the open sky, on the dirt, brimming with ideas and packed full of people who would delight in all the quirky things they were learning. Crijji could see them learning about the histories of other tribes, and experimenting with different substances, and building cars and motorbikes and in not too long even aeroplanes... He grinned when imagining familiar people cramming too many family members into the back of a smudgy-windowed space ship, from there taking off and chugging across the sky, leaving a thick black contrail all over its blueness.

It wasn't only hopeful stuff that Crijji visualised. Pressing heavily on his mind was something he'd repeatedly witnessed in his studies: the ineradicable lust for power. He feared his actions might heap logs onto a dormant flame, one that had never been able to grow because it didn't have the proper material. If Crijji was providing that material – knowledge – he could potentially conjure an insatiable bushfire. This made him wonder if he was wrong in his ambitions. Would his people be better off not knowing about the world beyond their own? Was he wrong to wipe the dust off the dividing glass wall, in the hope that future generations might develop the tools and the will to crack then shatter it? He didn't know. And maybe he never would.

Crijji's hardened feet walked over swelling hills and coiling sandy riverbeds, past Eucalyptus trees whose smell he would always from now be grateful for. Several days ago the language of the land had grown immediately comprehensible. He'd known the very moment when he'd entered familiar country.

The clouds in the westward sky were clumps and streaks of gold dissolving in a sea of apricot acid. The land beneath was a warped and crinkled expanse of dust and rock and isolation. The birds barely spoke, the air lost warmth, the stars were reappointed, and darkness cloaked the world.

Landmarks led Crijji to a campsite where six or seven scattered fires burned in the gloom. He could hear husky voices and humorous growls, animated conversation, and laughter. For days he'd fought off a welling sense of dread, suppressing it with any thought that might distract him. Now he was thoroughly drenched in dread, and fighting the impulse to run away from this place and return to the White Frick world. But he couldn't do that. His people needed to know: There were tribes they didn't know about, and one day those tribes would come – if not because of him, then eventually for another reason. Of that he was certain. Summoning every molecule of courage he possessed, Crijji took a step forward, and tipped himself over the edge of an inner precipice.

The forty or so members of his tribe were slouched or sitting cross-legged near the fires, eating kangaroo meat, telling funny stories, playing with babies, tending to weapons... Their many classes and categories registered to Crijji as he approached them. He saw men and boys he considered his fathers and fathers-in-law, women and girls he considered his mothers and mothers-in-law... there were men of the single man's camp, and women he couldn't speak to because of the marriage group they belonged to. Every single person had a totem declarative of the land they were conceived upon; a public name they were addressed by; and a secret name bestowed by the elders. They were either initiated adults or un-initiated children. Each was nested inside a rigid framework of associations: a social structure that would be dizzying to an outsider, but to Crijji was simpler than picking up a rock.

The chatter gradually diminished till nothing remained but silence. Every single person was looking at Crijji, who had stepped beyond the mulga trees and entered the light of the campfires. At first there was confusion. Then there was irritation. Then came anger. The change that followed was incredible. People cuter than teddy bears underwent an instant transformation that made their eyes gleam demonically. Crijji's tribe-members looked at him with such fierceness that a deep shiver took hold of his body. They pointed at him, saying he deserved to die, saying if he didn't the bad spirits would return to execute justice. Soon the women were screaming and the children were crying. People were shouting that the demons were coming. The men gripped their weapons and stalked toward Crijji. But Crijji had a plan.

In one hand was his glassy phone, scrunched up like a ball of dough. In the other hand was something he'd got Shaquille to buy him, several days before Shaquille had driven him to the ORAU border. When Crijji had first met

Albad, Albad's hair was a rainbow flame, courtesy of a cheap party device given to him by a White Frick. Crijji had remembered how scared he'd been in that moment. The memory of that fear had given him an idea.

Crijji had hold of a powder that erupted with crackling sparkles when he threw it up into the air. In the White Frick World this colourful stuff was nothing but a gimmick, but here it was evidence of powers above the natural. His people screamed in terror, their bodies paralysed save to shield their eyes. As the flashing dust continued with its tiny glowing explosions, Crijji slipped a minuscule device onto his own scalp. His hair immediately sprung up outwards and ignited with dazzling colours. The angry rainbow fire on top of his head so horrified people that he could barely hear himself shouting, *Ged im! Kill im! Payback! Dead! Ged im! Kill im! Payback! Dead!*

Over and over he yelled those key phrases, desperately hoping they were being perceived by the chips in people's hands. To purchase more time, he raised his arm high in the air, slid his thumb across his phone in a particular movement, and winced when the device lit up like a snow-coloured sun. His people were petrified by this magic stone suddenly revealed. It was proof of magic, proof of capabilities. Its pale form shimmered in their captivated eyes. Having entered their minds it would never be forgotten.

Waving his phone around to keep people's attention, Crijji traipsed carefully through the midst of his screaming tribe-members. Their bulging eyes denoted the fear lurking beneath their beliefs. Their breathing was so erratic it seemed their spirits had caught palsy. Even the elders were frightened by what Crijji had brought. Some of them raised their arms as if to hit the device, but jolted as though locked into place by an overriding instinct of restraint.

In spite of his object of power, Crijji was just as scared as everyone else. His skin seething, his stomach a toxic gob, he glanced repeatedly at the darkness beyond the spindly mulga trees, hoping that soon his helpers would arrive. His people needed to witness the full measure of his abilities. He could only show it by way of his protectors.

And finally they came.

From out of the deep shadows encircling the tribe emerged animals intent on achieving calm. Kangaroos and dingoes, emus, lizards and screeching birds, all of them otherworldly because none of them were real. They hopped, prowled, crawled, flapped, all looking inward toward the natives, whose horror reached an all new height.

The frenzy of the tribes-people reached its apex when King Brown snakes slithered across the red sand, their curling bodies carving wakes, their scales glistening in the light of the fires. Even though Crijji knew the serpents weren't real, they repulsed him so severely that he almost gagged. His next essential measure made him cringe when he thought about doing it. But if he didn't do it, his people would eventually doubt his connection to the animals, and his credibility would be questioned.

Amassing all of his determination, Crijji steeled himself and walked toward one of the closest snakes. It was standing upright, its front half off the ground, its compact head looking around with oil-drop eyes. Evidently the animals weren't sure about which person they were meant to be protecting. Each was looking about as if scanning the many faces. The snake saw Crijji coming and hissed. The sight of its open mouth made him want to shriek. Rather than doing that, he bent down, reached out, grabbed the snake by the throat, and lifted it off the ground. Swearing rang out on all sides of him. Screams continued to tear the night. The snake was light in his hands – lighter than he'd expected. He held up it as further evidence of his powers, juggling people's attention from the glowing stone in one hand to the serpent in the other. He could see that people believed him: men, women, children – even the elders. Crijji could see in their eyes that they knew: his power was unparalleled.

Ay! You mob! shouted Crijji, when the screaming and swearing had abated just enough for him to be heard. *Deez anmuls, I bin tell 'em come here, coz you all god lizzen. Out dere, long way way, dere's people, dey god magic, and dey bin tell me: I'll show youz ow use it. You wan fly, right up dere, I'll teaj you. Bu'choo god lizzen.*

The animals seemed to have entered a standby mode. They still roamed throughout the campsite to make known their authority, but their aggression seemed to focus on a place beyond the people.

Deez one, said Crijji, referring to the animals, *ip you get cheeky, dey'll gedjoo. En-one make trouble, dey'll come. Eeben ip I'm dead.*

Those words made the impression Crijji hoped they would. His people understood that attacking him would do no good. His magic would outlive him.

Now you mob all be quiet, and dey all go 'way. Coz memba: deez one look ahpter me.

Calmness so thick it was like a new atmosphere began to settle on the tribe. Hearts were still racing, and the slightest unexpected noise could destroy it, but it remained, a precarious stasis. The animals responded to the silence. Bowing their heads they turned away and departed, the kangaroos jumping, the dingoes scampering, the lizards crawling, the birds flying, and the snakes, the last to leave, slithering.

The snake in Crijji's hand was twisting its head around and writhing sinuously, its mouth wide open to show its horrible little teeth. As Crijji knelt down to place it on the dirt, the tip of its tail touched the ground and the rest of it curled up like a descending rope. Crijji let go of its throat and stepped backward, hopefully not betraying his fear of the fake reptile. It turned and looked at him, opened its mouth, and hissed. Crijji was repelled by the creature, and glad when it lowered its head and slithered away to follow all the other animals.

The silence was immense, broken only by the sound of logs popping and crackling in the campfires. Crijji's people continued to look at him fearfully. It took a few moments, but he remembered his head was still glowing with colour. Reaching up to his scalp, he pinched the device on top of it. His hair stopped glowing and fell down onto his face. Some people laughed, others yelped.

Spotting the closest child and walking over, Crijji reached out slowly and placed the device on the boy's head. The boy, who had shrunken in fear as Crijji approached, jumped in fright when everyone around him gasped or yelled out swear words. *His* hair now glowed like a rainbow fire. People laughed disbelievingly, and shortly there was a line to have a turn of the device. Crijji wondered if by explaining this little mystery he might be laying a foundation for chaos. He feared what could happen if his people learned too much too quickly; say if they learned his guardians were actually harmless. He could see them laughing as they smashed the robots for the fun of it, and himself standing back, powerless to stop them. Already this had happened in the Originals' timeline. For tens of thousands of years violence and the fear of it had preserved their way of life; and then had come a deposing authority that softened till it was laughable. Crijji would have to be cunning, and alert, to see that history didn't repeat itself. If it did, the result could again be disastrous.

That night, after Crijji had settled on the ground, near a fire, and told his people about where he'd been and some of the things he'd seen, he sat alone, in the quiet, and listened to everyone sleeping. Some had crawled into their wurlies – huts made of interlocking branches – to join a pile of sleeping family members. Others had remained by the fires. Crijji, with his arms around his knees, stared into the dwindling flames; and when breaking away from them, placed his eyes on the nearby children. He saw their little faces become warped and elongated, marred by the effects of foetal alcohol syndrome. He shivered to imagine such a thing, and knew the future could easily conjure it. Barely audibly, he spoke words from *Anthropia*:

Below the Self was laid a slab
For people yet to be
Their bodies laid out on it
In the shadow of the Tree

Was Crijji doing the same thing, in his effort to dig a new canal for the story of his people to flow down? Was he leading them toward an edge, and a spill that would develop into a thundering waterfall, all because *he* thought it was the right thing to do? He remembered how the crosses picked up and carried by the Humanists had been the abutments of a rising road to nowhere, the fall off the end of it spectacular. It was a dangerous business, trying to commandeer a narrative. They can prove far greater, and more unwieldy, than expected.

Buried without ceremony
No stone to mark its site
No lapidary chronicle
Of missing stars but grasping night
For the gold of which the coat was cast
(Mined from mere thought bubbles)
Was revealed as far more Wish than Rule
When their kind encounters troubles.

Crijji awoke to the present moment and looked around, not quite believing where he was. It had been such a long time since he'd lived among his people. Truly he'd thought he'd never get to see them again. But now here he was, in the land he belonged to, among the people he belonged to. He was relieved, happy, and grateful... but he was also wary. He was different to them now. The things he knew made him different. And because differences divide people, he would certainly encounter the Invisible Wall.

Crijji recalled the bristling, tingling resistance he would feel whenever pressing against the will of a tribe, be it here or in the White Frick world. Eventually he'd realised it wasn't the will of a tribe he was irritating; it was the will of a totem, which lives *through* a tribe. There's a thing called the *idea-ideal-idol* continuum, and through it, Thought flows into Deed, and Deed flows into Object. That the Object then flows into Thought makes it something of a cycle, one that, to Crijji's way of thinking, allows an immaterial thing to manifest in the material. These immaterial things that desire a fuller form, they don't like it when something impedes their manifestation, and they actively antagonise whatever might threaten it. This was why tides of *demon*strating angrivists had smothered anything regarded as defiant. As makers of worlds, totems fully recognise destroyers of worlds, and tell their possessions to eradicate such things, no matter how harmless they appear to be.

It was a deception that totems and people are one: that each is essentially the other. A totem merely *wears* people, like a skin, and is perfectly happy to slough its people off and roam around to find another skin. Crijji remembered all those individuals whose dogma collars had leashed them to a strangling ideal, and how they'd been the willing hands and feet of something that ultimately proved to regard them with contempt. The light they'd held up had not only blinded them to the darkness inside them, it had scorched them. And their totem... it had laughed. Crijji didn't know how he knew that. He just knew it.

The surrounding mulga trees were like emaciated dead corral, grey and blending with the night. Listening to the air being shredded by their leaves and branches, Crijji thought of the night when he'd left his tribe to build his subversive fires. As he'd stared at the stars above, waiting for some kind of response, he'd regretted his short-lived disbelief in devils, and was certain they'd influenced him to break the tribal law. It was funny. Of all the things he'd seen in the intervening time, nothing had contradicted the belief of his people: that bad spirits are real, and always whispering to make trouble.

The glowing rubble of the dying fire would soon be covered with ash. From the outside it would be a perfect picture of destruction, while inside it would thirst for resurrection. Peering at the inky realm beyond the trees, not with fear but with understanding, Crijji smiled without any kind of joy, and waited expectantly for the rising sun to destroy the darkness.

XXXII

Blue and gold, the sky and sun, there was nothing else directly above. Crijji sat on a hill and looked out across his country. Rugged to the point of barbarity, it reminded him of how the Originals had once been called the toughest people on the planet. And yet, said the same person, spindly-armed suburbanites and doughy generic worldlings considered themselves their defenders. What an insult, thought Crijji. But such is the power of numbers. The fact that Crijji's people were comparatively so few in numbers was perhaps cause to regard his plans as silly. That wouldn't stop him, though. In fact he didn't even think about it. Thoughts of futility could squash a person. That was why he'd stopped listening to the TRs. With all their talk of proudness, they simultaneously coated the Originals in subtle words of belittlement, making it seem they were frail and feeble, and desperately in need of someone else's help. The toughest people on the planet, thought Crijji, unable to keep from smiling. *That* was something to be proud of.

He remembered some of the Originals who had served in World War One, even though technically they weren't allowed to be soldiers. One group of White Fricks had tried to kick some of them out, but another group had said, If those blokes go, we go too. They were Light Horsemen, that mob; and Crijji admired them, particularly for how they'd realised the world was bigger than what they'd first thought; so had picked up new forms of weapons to protect their people. He sometimes wondered how those men – those warriors – would react upon seeing the HMAS Victimhood. Guaranteed they would raise their rifles, and take aim at every over-sized band-aid keeping it afloat.

Sketched upon Crijji's sky was an outline of a city that might potentially grow. He wondered if its myriad moving parts would prove too overwhelming for some people, and lock them out of the warmth it created. Would the Originals again feel out of sync with the world that had risen around them, even if this time it was a world they'd helped to create? Some probably would. Others would likely thrive. That seemed to be the way of things. People were all different, and they did things differently. This was why Crijji imagined little totem poles being raised across the landscape for as far as he could see, lifted up by one group, pushed over by another, swaying like the blades of barometers.

The arguments they measured would likely be comparable to those in the Divided Age. There'd be spectrums of racism-realism, privilege-proficiency, jealousy-injustice, intention-interpretation, freedom-fantasy... But whatever the labels of the gauges, their indicators would all be subject to the forces of a mega-totem – the macro object to the micro object nested in cortex vortexes. Operations to remove particular objects might in time be required, similar to the way that Crijji and Albad had cut the chips from their hands to move beyond the boundary lines. Then again, doing so might cultivate the chaos that the elders kept in abeyance, their rituals serving to ground people and keep them from floating away from each other.

Although in many ways Crijji's future efforts would siphon much power away from the elders, he was highly grateful for their governance. Without their upholding of sacred objects, solution would turn to dissolution, as had happened to the people who comprised the golden tree. Even though stone cathedral signal towers had pulsed out an ethos, and wizards with their upward waves had fanned the flames of fervency, the gravity bonding people had weakened till they'd all drifted away from each other. That outcome was sometimes attributed to a paradox that couldn't be processed. As the White Fricks had cleansed the Earth, pruning and taming their unruly species, giving to Anthropia the offerings that would have it rain its beneficence onto their soil, their deeds followed the framework of the Holy Post, an obelisk meant to guide the many vines of the human species, that they conform in their multiplicities to a sole direction and outcome. However, natural tendencies didn't follow the armature, and the gleam apportioned to inspire allegiance also manufactured a mental schism. The object was bright and shining, but at the same time wayward and self-absorbed. Opposing beliefs had created a short circuit. This created fragmentation.

Crijji often thought about the Mother, Dream, and Holy Post, whose symbiotic process reminded him of the Earth's magnetic field. The trio's energy, as he thought of it, flowed up through the idol, dispersed through Anthropia, then rained down onto the planet, where it was absorbed, and continued flowing as it had: up through the idol, out from Anthropia, and down onto the Earth, not only circulating, but intensifying. This intensification was described by the song *Deified and Reified*. Deify means: to regard something as a god, a god being a thing of supreme importance. Reify means: to make more real.

As something is continually charged with supreme importance, it becomes ever more real: collecting nutrients and building itself almost into a living thing. The thoughts directed toward an object can turn it into a kind of organism.

That people could be the veins supplying the blood of an invisible being was a thought that had many White Fricks scratching their heads, even though their species had performed that very action for thousands of years. In spite of Crijji's relative inexperience with theories and concepts, he found the idea easy to understand. Perhaps it was so clear because, as a totemite, he was categorised as an animist. Animism is where people consider objects, places and creatures to have a distinct spiritual essence. They see life in things that aren't strictly living.

Because his thoughts rested so heavily on the future, Crijji often imagined the emergence of a new ritualistic object. He thought of it rising out of the ground like a slow-moving geological mushroom cloud, disrupting the territories of many tribes, and ripening into an image whose features might not be determined for hundreds or even thousands of years. There would always be an image gathered around. That much was certain. Like the White Fricks, who had thought they were that Jesus bloke; and like totemites who think they're a particular animal, people will always charge something with a religious impulse, and adopt more of its characteristics the longer they look at it. Although he couldn't yet perceive the shape or features of the coming object, his understanding that ideas generate into ideals and then idols meant it was becoming as real to him as the rocks and trees, animals and sky. Again, that was animism shining through. He could almost see the totem rising from the ground, and breaking away to have a distinct life of its own. Like a dust particle it would attract moisture, and that moisture would develop into a rain drop.

If the new emerging image was anything like the golden tree, it would spit up pagans and puritans, rhetoricians and redeemers, all tinted a new shade courtesy of ideas from elsewhere, but sporting old characteristics because they were the output of an ancient brain. These people would draw their lines in the sand and strut around like soldiers, having no idea they were the servants of something immaterial. That was why Crijji had learned to look *beneath* the wriggling borderlines scrawled across the ground, to try and see the features *under* those flickering shadows. Each god - each object of supreme importance - has its own territory, gravity, and tribe; and if a person's eyes are well enough attuned, they can see a god's face bulging up from the terrain like a spectre waxing into the physical. The shining of light onto the faces of such beings... perhaps that was an ideal worth codifying.

Crijji imagined himself releasing lightbulbs that floated like balloons, and hands reaching out to either smash or grab them. The people who grabbed them could watch an approaching planet and hitch themselves to it. Those who smashed them would in turn be smashed – by a giant hurtling form that would strike them in their darkness. As Crijji thought about all the things he might be bringing into his land, he remembered a song from Anthropia, and quietly sang:

> *Bring your ways and be absorbed*
> *All ye children of the world*
> *May our forms unite to be as One*
> *That our potential be unfurled*
> *Those words were said as people came*
> *To rise just like a flame*
> *To overcome their differences*
> *And burnish their kind's name*
> *With able hands reaching up to seize*
> *A doubtless destiny*
> *And clean slate laid over blackened soil*
> *People worshiped true and free*
> *But this was only done until*
> *An old truth echoed loud:*
> *A tribe with*
> *all the gods it likes*
> *Is weaker than a shroud.*

All of those White Frick words Crijji understood now, thanks to the visual dictionaries that explained their meanings. The act of learning he found difficult. It was like pressing through an electrical fog that wanted to push a person ever backwards. But he knew: the more it was done, the easier and more satisfying it would become. He would impart that principle to anyone with the desire to know it. Little kids, especially. He often wondered what sort of minds would grow from a changed ethical soil, and what kind of songs and dances would fade away as the circle preserving each belief broke down. In sunny moments he saw pipes and irrigation, kangaroo farms and emu farms, and electrical light-shows splashing ancient stories across the night sky. In darker moments he saw wooden-stake compounds from which warlords sallied forth, and troops lined up in the thousands, marching as one to the beat of a didgeridoo. Whenever he felt he might be leading his people toward ruin, he would cheekily remind himself of a natural reality: A landscape might be blackened and seemingly destroyed, but then would come shoots of greenery, just as Liam had once said.

The huge fulsome clouds in the north-west were like powdery explosions frozen in time. Crijji wasn't sure if they were real or manufactured; where they were going or where they were from... but he knew they wouldn't stay where they were; and he knew they wouldn't stay as they were. They would roam all the Earth, dancing around each other, their songs echoing and crashing through every land, their bellies always threatening to break open and unleash the power trapped inside them. Not for the first time, Crijji thought that clouds were just like tribes. And clouds, of course, were water particles gathered around dust particles.

With a clearness of eye that he would always labour to keep, Crijji looked out across his country, watching red dust clouds rise off the ground like ghosts hoping for fuller life. He loved this land with everything inside him, and shuddered when remembering how his people's respect for it had been ridiculed, what with how the common indigenous group habitually left in its wake enough rubbish to recreate a fleet of Hindenburgs. Smashed cars and trashed houses, ever replenished in a cycle undisputed... It made him think of circular dances that raged across the land like dervishes, destroying, ever destroying, simply because a spirit wants to make trouble.

Crijji had decided; and on this matter he was immovable: if any pesky demon wanted to seize control of a tribe, and have it storming and stamping across the earth like a wild bushfire, he would do what that Original bloke Matthias Ullungara had done when he'd captured Australia's very first Japanese prisoner of World War II. He'd grab whatever was at hand, make out it was much more dangerous than it really was, and say, 'Stig 'em up. I'm Hobbalong Cazzidy.'

THE END

Don't miss out!

Visit the website below and you can sign up to receive emails whenever Courtney Taylor publishes a new book. There's no charge and no obligation.

https://books2read.com/r/B-A-HVQAB-WTMOC

BOOKS 2 READ

Connecting independent readers to independent writers.

Also by Courtney Taylor

Where the White Fricks are
Saint Wally
Ted Kelly: The Best Bloke Ever